THE EIGHTIES

The Eighties

Vinyl Tiger 2nd Edition

DAVE DI VITO

DDV

COPYRIGHT PAGE

DISCLAIMER

Disclaimer: The material in this book is for mature audiences only and contains graphic content.

It is intended only for those aged 18 and older.

The Eighties: Vinyl Tiger Second Edition is the updated version of *Vinyl Tiger,* originally published in 2015.

| 1 |

THE ASHRAM

"London is burning again," Shelly sighed.

Sitting at the window, she put her hand to her temples to try and stop the spinning. Although capable of spending whole days chain smoking, the smell of burning rubber outside had put her off her cigarette. She crushed it on the windowsill and tossed it down to the street, slamming the window closed.

"What? Why are you looking at me like that?" she asked, her voice even more gravelly than usual. "That cigarette butt is hardly going to make any difference. The city's already being torn apart, you know."

"Well good I say," Alex replied from the shaky card table, his hands pressed into his forehead. "Finally, something interesting going on."

"Surprised you even noticed," Shelly said, flopping down onto the newspapers on the beanbag, making a crunching sound. "What with *the big decision* and all. Have you made up your mind yet?"

Annoyed by her use of air quotes he simply shook his head.

He wasn't sure, but he doubted that he was ready for another change. It didn't matter to him that London was tearing itself apart. He still felt like he was a part of it, whatever it now was.

Alex did however, have some misgivings about his instincts. They'd sharpened over the years, even if they'd never proved much help when it came to dealing with the fallout heeding them brought. But for now, they were telling him to stay when they usually told him to run, just as they had two years ago.

Those two years had taken him a world away from his former self. From the kid who was always looking for a sign and who excelled at study, not because he was particularly gifted, but because he saw learning as a potential way out.

Back then, the old Alex considered Melbourne something of a ghost town. He knew there was nothing wrong with having values or a community spirit. It's just that he was never able to buy into many of the ideals his fellow Melbournians seemed to prize or obsess about. He spent much of his time there trying to suppress the nagging urge to get out and to play with danger. Back then, Alex felt surrounded by people looking for a calmer life, a fate he considered worse than death. Even his parents seemed to want an easier ride, constantly talking about the ways they avoided confrontation during their long working days. And though inheriting their work ethic had proved helpful at times, he loathed how their value system also crept into his thinking.

The last few months in London had been patchy. He'd experienced a few highs, but they'd been more than drowned out by the lows. Licking his wounds, the only comfort he took was in knowing that he wouldn't wind up anything like his siblings. He couldn't bear the idea of being like them, kitted out, as they were, in the drag and mannerisms of people twice their age. He felt they'd given up too easily, buying into the idea that life was a series of rites that they needed to work their way through: *Graduation. Employment. Marriage. A first home. Children.*

Alex had no doubt that they were making strides on life's big ladder while he was still stuck out on some weird tangent. But amidst all the chaos in London, he nonetheless felt like something was finally changing. People on the streets complained that nothing good could come from the rage sweeping through the city, but he disagreed. Even in the darkest times, he was sure he'd managed to catch glimpses of hope.

But now that he was being offered another out, he was having trouble finding the will. He'd had no trouble finding it the first time, even if he'd been short sighted about it all, having dismissed that first opportunity as a temporary distraction; a "trial escape" from life in his glorified country town.

That first out had literally landed in his lap while on a first year scholarship at university. The scholarship had already given him some freedom; on receiving the initial stipend, the first thing he did was move into a shared house in the inner city, which proved far more tolerable than life in the outskirts where he'd grown up.

That year he did whatever he could to exorcise his younger self, experimenting in all kinds of ways, determined to shed 'both of his virginities'. He dispensed with one with a girl at a campus party and the other with Angus. While nothing eventuated from the one–night stand at the party, something clicked between he and Angus, despite all the obstacles they faced in spending time together. It may have been the seventies, but Melbourne was no Utopia. And though Angus was married, the problem didn't rest with his wife, Maureen. Maureen knew about their arrangement and even fussed over Alex when he visited. The problem partly stemmed from not being able to be seen in public together. As a university lecturer, Angus had a reputation to protect. So regardless of what Angus and Alex felt for each other, there were social norms that needed to be respected and they had to conduct their relationship on the down-low.

Angus had made short work of seducing Alex. He'd noticed Alex and his broad build early in the academic year. Angus had enjoyed how the boy seemed to look at him, Alex's caramel eyes lingering at the lectern longer than necessary. On multiple occasions, Angus also noted how Alex was slower to pack up his things than the other students. How Alex always had a question or a comment he wanted to make once the lecture was over.

It had been easy enough to convince Alex to volunteer for him and have Alex come to his office every week to help with the filing or to run errands around campus. And it had proven just as simple, one Friday afternoon, to corner the lad next to the unwieldly philodendron in Angus' tiny office. To get Alex onto his knees while Angus unbuttoned his slacks and watched the boy work with gusto as Angus added a very intimate chore to Alex's list of things to do.

Alex for his part, ignored his classmates when they gossiped about Angus. He didn't care for their innuendos about the professor, even if it stung to know that he wasn't the first guy Angus had taken under his wing.

Still, exploring sex with Angus was mostly turning out to be exhilarating. Angus might have been unflappable at uni; relaxed, easy going, even approachable, but he was different in the bedroom. He seemed more intense, routinely barking instructions and saying unspeakable, horrid things in the heat of the moment, before he'd climax noisily and then revert to his calmer, more collected self, who would then lavish Alex with praise.

There were times where Angus' sexual requests seemed outlandish to Alex, but he didn't want to disappoint. Alex couldn't have Angus thinking he was a prude, so he gave himself over completely, doing everything that was asked of him. It was only on his way home afterwards, lost in his own thoughts, that Alex would begin the downward spiral, wondering whether he'd gone too far and if Angus' other acolytes had been as prepared to please the professor as he was. It was a doubt that constantly plagued him.

Considered a disadvantaged student at the country's most prestigious university, Alex knew that he had to work harder than everyone else to prove his worth. While many of his classmates spent their semester breaks vacationing, Alex spent his doing volunteer stints in the copy room at a local newspaper and taking nightshifts bussing tables at a recently opened eatery.

On a rainy Sunday morning after a particularly gruelling shift, he woke to the sound of his irritated housemate.

"It's for you," the housemate groaned from the door.

"What?" Alex asked, groggily sitting up in his bed.

"The phone. Someone for you."

It was unlike Angus to call on a Sunday and they hadn't spoken in a fortnight. Angus apologised profusely for having been away at conferences in Canberra and Newcastle before asking Alex to make the trek over to his house in one of Melbourne's leafier suburbs.

After being ushered in, Alex left his waterlogged boots at the entrance and followed Angus down the airy hallway.

"Here," Angus said, handing Alex a pair of slippers. "Put these on and I'll make you a cup of tea. Go and have a hot shower and I'll bring it in to you."

Once he'd showered, Alex wondered whether he should wait in the bedroom or not. His clothes were still wet, so he put on a t–shirt he found hanging on the back of the bathroom door and hung his own clothes to dry near the radiator.

"Maureen's in Sydney. She's at a conference," Angus said, waltzing into the bedroom and handing Alex a steaming hot mug.

Alex sat up in the bed, pulling the covers up before sipping his tea.

"Is she well?" Alex asked, steadying his grasp of the mug as Angus briskly undressed on the bed and dived under the covers.

"She's fine," Angus said dismissively. "Alex, what's your view on ashrams?"

"I think we've spoken about them before, haven't we?"

"Have we? Well, will you humour me on this shitty, rainy day?"

"Well, they only exist to make wealthy people feel better about themselves, don't they? To make them feel like they're in on some secret."

Angus chuckled. "Tell me more," he said, running his hand through Alex's damp, peroxided hair.

"Well, it's the stuff of hoary old rich people and hippies, right? People who have time to kill. You don't hear the average Joe bragging about how they spent a week folded up like a pretzel, do you?"

Angus chuckled again. "Just as Maureen predicted. You know she thinks I've got a thing for cynics."

"Is it true?" Alex asked, setting the mug down.

"Could well be," Angus smiled. "Speaking of Maureen, she agreed to my proposal. That you come with us," he said, stretching his arm around Alex's shoulders.

"Come with you? Where?" Alex asked, detecting a hint of musk radiating from Angus' armpit.

"To India. We've booked a month on a retreat there. I want you to come with us. *We* want you to come."

"Not to an ashram I hope," Alex said.

"It could be good for you," Angus said, pulling Alex closer, the hum of Angus' deep voice reverberating through Alex's body. "And if it's not your thing, there's a whole country to roam. An entire subcontinent. It could be just the thing to inspire you for all those design projects you're always telling me about."

Alex looked at him suspiciously.

"I couldn't afford it. Even if I did want to come, which I don't."

"Maureen also said you'd say something like that. And she wanted me to tell you that as our guest, we'll pay for your trip."

Alex felt something uncomfortable stirring in his gut, but Angus' enthusiasm was endearing.

"We've got a bunch of friends we meet there every year and they'll be there, but I really want you to come along. Partly to say thanks for everything you do for me at work, but also because I think we'll have a ball there."

"Won't it be weird for you? Or for Maureen? Having me there like that?"

"Not at all. You're important to us. She loved the idea of inviting you along," Angus said, his fingers exploring the undercarriage of Alex's privates.

"Besides, one of her special friends is flying in for the month too. Promise me you'll at least think about it."

That evening, over a family dinner in the suburbs, Alex announced that he'd been invited to travel abroad.

"For a yoga retreat. Meditation, excursions into an old Raj town… that kind of thing," he explained, clumping the cannelloni onto his fork.

He expected someone to be excited for him. To congratulate him. But instead, his family looked at him like he was mad. Only Domenic, Alex's brother, seemed prepared to actually verbalise what he was thinking.

"You better not do anything to jeopardise your scholarship, Alex. Mum and dad have made so many sacrifices for you. You're the only one of us that's been given the chance to go to uni."

The idea of throwing everything away hadn't even occurred to Alex. He'd never disguised the fact that he was looking for a ticket out of Melbourne, but obviously one to a global capital, not an abandoned Maharaja villa somewhere in the Indian countryside.

The Sunday dinner quickly descended into its usual mix of accusations and insults. Perhaps his family knew something about him that he didn't, that they knew him better than he was prepared to admit. He'd only told them because he wanted to brag a little, but their contempt for the idea suddenly made accepting Angus' invitation a no brainer.

****

He'd never been on a plane before, let alone one to another country. And though friends warned him to expect some unfamiliarity and disorientation on arriving in India, Alex didn't think he'd still feel so depleted days into his trip.

Initially he attributed his wooziness to jetlag and to the embarrassment of feeling out of his element, what with all the new company he was keeping. Though Angus had told him they would be meeting friends, it transpired that the ashram was simply full of return visitors, only some of whom Angus and Maureen were actually friendly with.

True to Angus' word, Maureen had disappeared off the radar with her German friend and the ashram proved just as beautiful as Angus had said it would be. The parched, terracotta coloured landscape struck Alex as did the retreat's main building, adorned as it was with domes and turrets. Alex spent most of his days sketching, only occasionally participating in the yoga workshops, which he was horrified to discover, he actually enjoyed.

But it was hard to maintain his energy levels in the stifling heat of the day. His breathing would only return to normal once the cooler air of the evenings arrived. It was only then that he could finally relax, briefly able to enjoy the retreat's cocktail hour before descending into his nightly wooziness. Though he could still function and interact, he felt his perception of what he saw or did in the evenings was being altered by a thick veil. The sensation would only lift in the mornings when he'd wake bleary eyed as the bright sun bounced around the walls of his room, emptying the tiny bungalow of what little air circulated inside it.

His disorientation was only compounded when he woke up in other people's rooms. Sometimes he'd find himself in Angus' expansive cottage style lodgings, but occasionally, Alex would also awaken in Angus' Welsh friend's bungalow, which was much like his own, only bigger.

Wherever he came to, Alex would begin the same daily ritual of splashing water onto his face and spending his morning trying to remember details from the night before.

The ashram was clearly a place where things worked differently. But after more than ten days of constantly being in a stupor, Alex began to worry. Those around him dismissed what he was feeling, attributing his body's sluggishness to low blood pressure or acclimatisation. The sheer frustration he had with their dismissals led Alex's street smarts to finally kick in.

Despite routinely turning down Angus' offers of various illicit substances, Alex began to suspect someone was slipping something into his food or drink. He had no proof, but from comments he heard from Angus and the Welshman, he gleaned the threat of being drugged was something of a running joke between them. When confronted, both flatly denied any wrongdoing, but Alex was sure there was more to his constant grogginess than jetlag alone. Yet even Alex initially had trouble convincing himself that the men were drugging him. At least until he began waking up to the uncomfortable sensation of feeling soiled.

The first time that happened, he feared that he was simply rundown or that he might have succumbed to Delhi belly. But after yet another long, hot day of being ignored by the men, who were increasingly annoyed by Alex's indirect accusations, Alex was determined to get to the bottom of things when they set their sights on him again in the evening.

Although unsteady, that night he remembered Angus and the Welshman helping him into Angus' suite. He'd felt a vivid rush when he realised he was soon kneeling on the bed with Angus, who was slowly kissing and undressing him as the Welshman watched from an armchair. Alex felt his awareness come and go, it only sharpening again at the sensation of the Welshman's wet breath on the back of his neck. From then on, the nightly veil fluttered like a curtain in the wind, permitting him only the briefest of glimpses into what they were doing. And then, it was as if all the lights went out.

When a draught of cold air surged through Angus' suite shortly after 2am, Alex awoke, his eyes quickly making an inventory of the three dim lamps that were still on in the room. Looking down, he found himself lying between the men. Angus' naked body and long legs commandeered much of the mattress, while the Welshman's seemed to hover at its edge.

Trying to sit up, Alex felt acute pain and discomfort all over. Looking down, he noticed his arms and chest were littered with red blotches. He detected an unpleasant smell, and, instinctively, sniffed his chest, immediately repulsed by the stench it gave off.

As he sat up carefully, the mattress and sheet beneath him felt damp and soft even if he felt stiff and achy. He looked at the men flanking him, and concentrated, trying to see beyond their doughy forms and greying body hair to remember what had happened before he'd lost track of events.

Beyond the din of their snoring, he remembered something. He remembered how intoxicating it had felt when Angus had joined him on the bed, kissing him so passionately. How Angus had then whispered something into his ear, the words all moist.

"Trust me," he'd said, Angus' deep voice sending another charge through Alex which repeated itself when he playfully bit Alex's earlobe.

Alex looked at Angus and his pale, freckly torso and then turned his attention to the Welshman who he'd instinctively disliked from day one. Staring at the Welshman's back, Alex was dragged back into his memory, with an abrupt flashback to the hard slaps made to his arse and to the back of his head, and of the orders being barked at him.

"Turn around!" the deep voice had bellowed.

He recalled obeying. Remembered taking both men into his mouth like he'd been ordered to. Remembered struggling to breathe, and how, when he did try to come up for air, he'd been admonished with two quick blows to the face. How that had sent a surge of panic through him that made him want to jump off the bed, which in turn made them restrain him, resulting in him being pinned down by the flabby Welshman. Angus' friend didn't care that Alex's head was throbbing as the blood rushed to it, it hanging uncomfortably over the edge of the mattress, hovering above the tile floor.

And when Angus hurriedly jammed it in, Alex wasn't sure they heard him yelp. He could only hear the Welshman goading Angus not to let go too soon. As the weight of Angus' body lifted off Alex, it was replaced by the Welshman's who announced his arrival with another hard blow to Alex's temple. Before Alex could even think of fighting back the Welshman had rolled him over, spreading Alex's legs and entering him in one foul swoop, instantly ploughing away.

Alex could see the ceiling fan but couldn't focus on it because there were other things competing for his attention. Like the horrible, dry burning sensation where the Welshman was pounding at him and the awkward feeling of warm liquid trickling down from Angus, which was pooling at Alex's clavicle and on the mattress below. And it was then that Alex remembered he'd closed his eyes to think about the terracotta red and the cool air before everything went black.

Now that he was awake again and lucid, his mouth was burning and his lips felt crusted at their edges. He didn't want to open his mouth lest he scream and wake them. Wanted to. Wanted to do unspeakable things to them or to maim them with whatever he could find in the room. But he told himself to focus on getting out of there.

He rose from the bed and limped over to the armchair and the desk. Keeping an eye on the bed, his anger authorised him to rifle through their belongings. From the wallets in the trouser pocket and the bedside drawer he took nearly all the cash they had, confident the amount was warranted by what he'd endured.

He put on his shorts, silently chastising himself for being so stupid for not having seen things sooner. He turned to check on them again and crept out of Angus' bungalow, making a dash in the darkness to his own where he quickly threw his belongings into his suitcase. Securing it with its leather toggles, he tiptoed to his door to check that there was no activity coming from Angus' bungalow. Satisfied there wasn't, he strapped on his backpack and picked up his suitcase, bundling it to his chest and ran into the silence.

He ran in parallel to the long gravel pathway that connected the villa to the main road. He figured it would be less noisy, even if he was terrified of ending up face down in a ditch. Once he reached the road he took a few breaths, trying to remember which direction he needed to head in. Deciding to go left, he sprinted in the almost complete darkness, relieved when he finally saw the beacon offered up by a tiny roadside stall in the distance. As he got closer, he almost let out a cheer when he saw a small group of rickshaw drivers loitering outside the store. He ignored their initial jeers and beseeched them to take him away; to the 'station': the place he'd alighted from less than a fortnight before. It seemed like none of them wanted the crazy, dishevelled white guy's fare. Not at that hour. But when Alex made eye contact with the youngest guy in the group, he reluctantly nodded in agreement to Alex's pleas. Alex divided his attention between the road that he'd run down and the kid who couldn't have been more than fifteen or sixteen years old, desperate for the teen to finish his snack and let him climb aboard.

At the station Alex spoke with the lone attendant in the ticket booth, gleaning that the first train was due in less than two hours. He bought himself a ticket to the last stop and was cautiously leaving the ticket office when his own reflection in the window stopped him in his tracks.

In desperation, he trawled the station grounds, and in the darkness behind a kiosk, found what he was looking for. He fumbled through his backpack for his bar of soap and crouched under the trickling faucet. He did his best to lather wherever he could reach, ignoring the cold air and the icy water as he contorted his body under the tap for as long as it took to feel sufficiently clean. Drying off, the urge to burn his small towel came over him, but instead he discarded it in the bushes and quickly got dressed.

Limping across the station grounds, he found a tiny nook on one of the platforms between a vendor and a grimy wall, content that he could see the station's comings and goings from there.

The vendor didn't seem to appreciate the company, growling something at him, but moments later he handed Alex a fried pastry and a soft drink, neither of which Alex recognised. As his body responded to the first hit of sugar and the energy it had been wringed of, Alex gratefully sought out a note from his loot. Unable to decipher the rupees in the low light, he settled instead on a $20 note which he folded into the vendor's fist, grateful tears coming to his own eyes when he saw the vendor break into a toothy smile.

As his mind counted down to the train's arrival, still over an hour away, he wondered whether it had all been a huge mistake on his part coming to India, getting caught up in a game beyond his abilities and then abruptly leaving the room like that. Was he simply overreacting to a night that had gotten out of hand? Perhaps the problem was his. Perhaps he wasn't as progressive and daring as he thought he was. Maybe he'd been naïve not to understand what the invitation had meant in the first place.

And what would he do if Angus and the Welshman turned up at the station before his train arrived? What if they made a scene and demanded all their money back? He had none of his own and a return ticket that was still nearly two weeks away from being useable.

But it hurt to think, let alone to sit, so he leaned his head against the wall and propped his bottom up so that it wasn't bearing any of his weight. And from that uncomfortable position, almost more yogic than his entire time at the ashram had been, he kept an eye on both the station clock and the iron entry gate.

As he waited nervously, he realised he hadn't really been at an ashram. Perhaps it was one in name, but really, it was just another place where privilege and hierarchies thrived, their dubious natures camouflaged by all the bright designer active wear.

As his anger subsided slightly, humiliation took its place. Looking around the station, the dusty setting only made him feel lonelier. He wanted to sleep and to forget about everything, but he knew he had to keep his wits about him. And after struggling to wade through another post–Angus downward spiral, it was with immense relief that he watched the rusty, noisy train finally pull into the station.

On the train people were transfixed by him. They marvelled at his (bleached) blond hair, his luminescent skin and the contradictions of his Eurasian face.

After an hour or so of traveling in relative darkness, it occurred to him that people were staring simply because he was something different to look at. No doubt they'd been cooped up in their compartments for hours. The news that a foreigner was on board also brought out visitors from the other carriages, some of whom tugged at his hair and dared to caress his skin.

In one of the lulls in interest, a Sikh sitting opposite Alex explained that vendors would soon enough be climbing aboard with chai and that people's attentions would turn elsewhere.

"Do you want some water? You look thirsty," the Sikh noted.

Alex wasn't sure he should accept. Maybe it was better to steer clear of other people's drinks, even if he was dying of thirst. But when the Sikh insisted, Alex thanked him.

"Where are you from?" the Sikh asked, pouring water into an aluminium cup.

"Australia," Alex said, knowing the answer was as out of place as he was.

"Australia? What are you doing here?"

"I'm on holiday," Alex whispered.

"Are you enjoying it?" the Sikh asked, spinning the flask cap closed.

Alex thought about how the only thing he'd seen in the country in the last fortnight had been every square inch of those middle-aged bodies.

"India is beautiful," Alex replied, looking out the window, thankful for the slither of light now streaming into the carriage. A light so soft, it almost made the train not seem like a cage on rails.

| 2 |

BOMBAY

Within a week Alex was teaching English at an orphanage in a hill station. Days after getting off the train, he'd been approached by someone on the street who had offered him the job. Absurd as it seemed, Alex felt it would be a good way of regrouping before deciding whether or not to fly home on the same flight as Angus and Maureen.

The governor of the orphanage arranged for Alex to move in with a British born Indian named Anesh, the only other foreigner in town. With a room to call his own, time slowly restarted for Alex.

At home and in the orphanage, Anesh and he quietly got to know one another, whittling away their nights reading or with Anesh teaching Alex how to play the acoustic guitar.

From the outset, Alex sensed Anesh's loneliness. Anesh never complained about it, but it was written all over his face.

Alex learned he'd been in town for two years now, and that the kids occupied much of his time and thoughts.

Though he found Anesh sweet, Alex rebuffed his clumsy advances, careful however, not to hurt his feelings. But after a couple of months of their shared solitude, Alex began to relent, no longer putting up resistance when Anesh asked for a hug. Eventually he even let Anesh sleep beside him some nights, the two occasionally engaging in some light petting. But Alex drew the line anytime it seemed things were about to go any further.

Although theirs was a relationship built around friendship and some harmless flirting, the familiarity and the pointlessness of their arrangement began to get to Alex after a couple of months. The charm of the tiny, fragrant hill town, which had served as such a wonderful refuge, also wore off, suddenly unbearably small and claustrophobic. Alex knew it had been bound to happen, but the suddenness with which the experiential use by date arrived surprised even him, as did the fact that Anesh seemed genuinely relieved when Alex announced he was leaving. And despite the remorse Alex felt for his group of children, he promptly left town one night without saying goodbye to them, because, he reasoned, the last thing they needed was someone else kissing them off.

His restlessness and the Indian train system transported him from the lush, high altitudes to New Delhi, where, before looking for lodgings, Alex sought out a hairdresser to cut and dye his two-toned hair. He settled for a plucky hairdresser near the main station who rendered his hair a shade of plum red, promising a circumspect Alex that it was the most popular colour among his clientele.

After a few weeks exploring the city and collecting random Hindi pop records, he still had a wad of ashram compensation cash, and with some of it, bought himself a one way train ticket to Bombay.

Careful to conserve what money he had left, Alex hit the pavement in search of work, quickly landing a job at a somewhat infamous expat bar. He spent long days bussing tables and bartending, regularly fending off the innuendos of the group of gay expats who made some shifts a living hell, even if they were generous tippers. Weeks into the gig, and seated at one of the outdoor tables on his break, Alex was sure he was being watched by one of them. So when a man walked over and complimented Alex on his unusual appearance, asking if he could join him, Alex gave him a polite, but firm *'no'*. But when the man made it clear why his interest in Alex wasn't romantic, Alex's expression changed and he invited the Chinese American to sit down.

"Don't get your hopes up," the man said, seeing Alex's face light up at the word *modelling*. "I may be a legitimate talent scout, but this is India after all. People who work with us only do it for pocket money." he said.

The scout gave Alex his card and the directions to his hotel, where they arranged to meet after Alex's shift. In the swank hotel room, effortlessly more stylish than Alex's lodgings at a guest house, the scout photographed Alex against a wall, showing him the photos before scribbling something over them in kanji. Though Alex was excited by the entire process, the scout seemed quite matter of fact about things and even briefly ignored Alex to attend to some paperwork.

"You can go now," he said from his desk. "I've got what I need. Just make sure you're downstairs in the foyer at eight thirty tomorrow morning."

The next morning, Alex crossed town as instructed. Arriving early, his knees almost gave way when he saw two extraordinarily beautiful giants loitering near the talent scout.

Alex nervously introduced himself to them when the Svengali failed to, doing his best to calm his nerves with small talk in the minivan on the way to their gig. The small talk revealed little more than the guys' names (Yevron and Adi) and their nationalities (Israeli and German). Neither of the giants seemed to know where they were all headed, both only having become 'models' in the last forty–eight hours, each discovered by the scout while walking Bombay's busy streets.

At ten a.m. they were ushered into a warehouse and made to strip down to their underwear as a steady succession of staff arrived with outfits for them to try on. None of the boys knew much about fashion, yet it was clear to them that they wouldn't be working with high end clothing.

But their likenesses as captured that day, wound up on the awnings of tailor shops across the subcontinent. The kinds that lure travellers in with the promise of a quick, cheap tailormade outfit. Even today, a walk through the marketplaces of some Indian cities still offers a glimpse of the boys' toothy grins and amateur poses.

But this was only the first of a series of jobs they had lined up. After a twelve hour working day, Alex spent the night at Adi's, whose hotel was much closer to the talent scout's than Alex's residence. And at the crack of dawn the next day, the minivan took them to an entirely different part of the city where the clothes were better made but the photo shoot was longer and more demanding.

Alex listened intently to the instructions, doing his best to understand what the photographer asked of him. During a break, while Alex and Adi watched with envy as Yevron was called back to work alone with the photographer's crew, the Svengali came and sat with them.

"He's very good at it isn't he?" he asked, the boys nodding.

"A real shame. He has visa problems, so he'll be finishing up in a few days. Listen boys, I have another client looking for some more male models. Mostly catalogue stuff but also some small ad campaigns."

"In Bombay?" Adi asked.

"No. In Tokyo."

Adi and Alex looked at each other and at the Svengali in disbelief.

"Don't get too excited. I know I said Tokyo, but it's not like the Tokyo you're probably imagining. Anyway, we can get the paperwork ready for you in about a week and the deal includes the flight. You just need to say yes."

That week Alex and Adi hung out together after bidding farewell to Yevron, who they'd dubbed *"the competition"*. Despite all the stimulation that Bombay offered, Alex felt his days with Adi were happily grounding. It was a relief to have someone to buffer everything around him and to be in the company of someone who wasn't at all jaded. As they got to know each other, Adi spoke of his life back at home; of his girlfriend, the family business and of his intent to enrol at university.

So it took Alex by surprise then, when back in their now shared hotel room for their last night in India, Adi silently leant in and kissed him. Alex hadn't seen it coming, even if it had proven a welcome surprise. At first, Adi's chapped lips had felt like sandpaper, the sensation made worse by the knowledge that Alex was kissing a friend. But the longer they kissed, the more Alex's focus was shifted by the soft, playful way in which Adi used his tongue. The tickling sensation set off a mass of butter-flies in Alex's stomach, they blindly ricocheting into the walls of Alex's abdomen like balls on a squash court.

As they kissed, Adi's hand crept slowly around Alex's torso, his fingers running along Alex's collarbone before converging to pinch at Alex's nipples. Adi's exploration had set off the de-sired reaction elsewhere and soon enough Adi's hand was down at the rim of Alex's jeans ready to explore. The shock of feeling Adi's hand suddenly down by his navel caught Alex off guard, and he felt himself freeze, unable even to continue kissing. His mind abandoned the moment, dragging Alex back instead to the ashram, a place and time Alex had spent months hiding from. But beyond the fog and that unpleasant sensation of dry, sharp air, Alex heard Adi repeating his name.

"Are you alright? We can stop if you don't want to do this," Adi said.

"I'm sorry, I just got a bit lost," Alex said, sitting up.

Adi studied him, looking deep into his eyes.

"Is something wrong?" Adi asked.

Alex decided he shouldn't answer. Instead he looked into Adi's eyes, sensing a softness in them that he wasn't accustomed to seeing. He'd never seen the same thing in Angus' eyes. And with that realisation, Alex smiled. He realised he needed to relax.

And anyway, he was almost certain he could trust Adi.

***

In Tokyo, the boys were ushered into an apartment complex near Koganei in the city's far west.

Looking at a map of the city, Koganei seemed a world away from Ginza, where Alex had heard all the foreign models lived. They'd heard that modelling in Japan was a 'dream gig', but soon enough their experience of working in India replicated itself in Tokyo's industrial belt.

After hours in the minivan each morning, crisscrossing freeways and anonymous suburbs, the boys spent their days trying to make sense of the things the photographers would say. Worse still, the boys had been housed with another "model" whose favourite pastime seemed to be complaining about how horrible working in Japan was.

Although their work schedules sometimes separated them, for much of their three months there, Alex and Adi still managed to explore Tokyo together in their down time. This often meant curtailing their nights out to catch the last train home, or, if schedule permitted, simply pulling an "all-nighter" and returning to the apartment with the morning's first trains.

"Have you been saving any money?" Adi asked Alex on one of the dawn train rides.

"Yeah. I don't know if it's enough, but I should be able to keep going for a while."

"Good. They told me yesterday that they won't be renewing my visa. So I'm going back home to Germany," Adi said.

Alex nestled his nose into Adi's nape, devouring the smell of baby shampoo. They'd taken to using it because it was the only brand that either of them recognised and both were too embarrassed to ask for a more adult alternative.

"Are you going back to Germany because you want to get out of the 'purgatory of low cost modelling'? Before it's too late?" Alex asked.

"Oh my God, our roommate really is a nightmare. Who talks like that? What about you? Have they said anything to you?"

"Not yet. But even if they do, I don't know if I want to go back to Melbourne. My family think I should. They keep saying how shocked they are that everything is somehow paying off. The last time I spoke to my mum, she reminded me that 'holidays have to end, otherwise they're not holidays, are they?'"

"She has obviously never worked for a budget modelling agency," Adi replied.

When their visas were about to expire, both boys were given their marching orders and their passports back.

"Let's not do our goodbyes in Koganei," Adi said. "We should go somewhere. Like Kyoto. We can get our flights out of Osaka. Seems a shame to be in Japan for so long and not see anything else."

With some effort, they convinced someone at the agency to make the arrangements for them. On their last day in Tokyo, their Svengali dropped by to say goodbye, accompanied by two new arrivals who would take their places at the apartment.

The boys then spent three days soaking up the atmosphere in the old imperial capital, whose record stores Alex scoured for

J–pop and *enka* when Adi wasn't dragging him in and out of the city's temples and historical sites.

"Are you sure you don't want to come to Hamburg?" Adi asked on their last full day together. They were sitting in the grounds of Kiyomizu temple watching the tourists shuffle along its pathways. "I'm going to miss having you around."

"I just think London is going to be easier for me," Alex said. "Even if I have no idea what I'm going to do there."

"You'll work it out," Adi said, putting his arm around Alex's waist. "At least you won't have to work in the family business like me."

"Promise me you'll keep an eye out for something else Adi. That you won't give up. I couldn't bear to think of you rotting away like that."

"I won't. I'll be fine, but you make sure you look after yourself too. London isn't all that people make it out to be."

| 3 |

LONDON

In London, Alex found modelling was no longer an option for him, despite his reasonably impressive portfolio. In London, Asia, where things had come so easily to him, suddenly seemed so far away.

"Too edgy", "too ethnic", "too short".

The British agents' words differed but the sense was always the same. Basically every one of his insecurities laid bare and verbalised. Whispered, of course, but said in firm belief.

Each time the tweed clad pterodactyls dismissed him from auditions and casting calls, Alex understood that little bit more that he needed to pursue other avenues.

He found a room in a house with four others and worked bussing tables, waiting, and occasionally doing some life modelling at an art college.

The art college doubled as his own personal marketplace. It was there he picked up occasional lovers, some paid design work and a second–hand guitar.

He could barely remember any of the things that Anesh had taught him but daily guitar practice helped him fill the gaping holes in his "work" schedule.

Although he was working like a dog and getting paid fuck all, he was content. Things were uncertain, but they were also fun, especially in the shared house that was falling apart at the seams.

By virtue of his housemates' and his own outgoingness, he began to move in more rambunctious circles. The new people, the occasional drugs and the ever–present music all helped him forget that he was starting from scratch again.

With time, Alex also achieved different forms of notoriety.

To some he was the guy who designed record sleeves on the cheap for their punk and rock bands. To others he was the guy in the underground clubs that was impossible to ignore, modelling the outlandish outfits of his designer friends from the art college.

In time, he also wrangled modestly paid dance and DJ gigs at many of the places he was already a fixture in. And as such, life in London inched him closer to what he imagined it should look like.

"You know," Shelly said, "I don't know how you keep it up. You must've done at least double time this week at the restaurant. And look at you. You're wearing nothing but a fig leaf and a pair of Dr. Martens, for god's sake."

"Yeah, but that pharmacist over there wouldn't have spoken to me if I wasn't dressed like this."

"You're not dressed. You're practically naked. Can't you take a night off from everything? I'm worried about you."

"Don't be. Anyway, he's taking me to a fancy lunch tomorrow. Thank God for Sundays."

Shelly called herself an artist whenever she met somebody, but Alex knew that she, and pretty much everyone he knew couldn't ever really back up such grand claims. They were presences on London's underground scene, but their dreams were confined to the walls of the clubs, gay bars and private parties that they frequented. These were the kinds of places where Alex was noted as much for his skimpy outfits as he was for the riotous DJ'ing work he did with his Asian music collection.

But beyond that world, Alex and his friends were subject to all kinds of derision. Their flamboyance didn't sit well with the gritty times. And his campy presence seemed to dare Londoners to stare and make comments, even if people alleged being queer was no longer the taboo it once had been.

Eventually though, the bottom even fell out of the underground. Money got tighter and tighter even at his more conventional gigs. Things got so bad in London that many of his friends considered moving away from the city just to keep afloat.

Kicked out of their squat, he and Shelly temporarily camped out on friends' living room sofas and floors until they availed themselves of another, this time on the edge of Kensington with another friend, Marin. Alex would call the squat home for the rest of his time in London.

Even with a "borrowed" roof over his head, times were tough, and necessity led to some of his life modelling to morph into nude modelling for a few soft porn rags here and there.

And though it probably would've been easy enough to take the step into the world's oldest profession, the one time he did straight out fuck for money didn't seem worth the paltry £15 his client paid him afterwards.

So as the financial crunch tightened, Alex settled instead for private life modelling sessions with a handful of regulars with whom he was sometimes prepared to take things further.

Alex hated those sessions, but beyond the pocket money they offered, they also meant having somewhere to have a hot shower or a decent meal to break up the monotony of his tin food diet in the draughty, glorified bedsit that he and the girls had commandeered.

All the while, he, his guitar and the sheet music he picked up were inseparable. He practiced the staples and old classics re-peatedly, much to the girls' chagrin. But Shelly's boyfriend, a gui-tar virtuoso, was happy for the musical company, even if it was inferior.

After a particularly tough six month run where Alex had dropped towel almost weekly, someone he met at one of his few DJ gigs (which he worked under the moniker of *Vinyl Tiger*; a nickname he'd earned along the way), asked if he might be inter-ested in working afternoons at a record store.

At the interview, the store manager interrogated him, check-ing to see if Alex could reel off the names of all the old Stooges albums or if he knew who Iannis Xenakis was. By virtue of the things he'd learnt from the people he hung around with, rather than through his own innate, eclectic taste, Alex managed to an-swer enough of the questions correctly to be hired on the spot.

Despite the manager's insistence that it was a serious record store for collectors, customers rarely asked Alex about obscure records. They seemed to be more interested in Blondie's *Parallel Lines* or the Buzzcock's *Love Bites*. The store also turned out to be something of a cruising ground. With a glint in their eyes, a sub-category of clients would ask for Grace Jones' *Fame* album or for the latest Andrea True release. Alex made a point of accompanying the better looking ones to the disco section. And at times, those few paces were sufficient to get the ball rolling.

Conversations inevitably included tried and true lines like *'have we met before?'* or *'you're so and so's friend right?'* but Alex truly engaged when the customers asked if it was him *'dancing at Sombrero's the other night?'*

On one particularly slow afternoon, Alex spied a thirty something guy flicking through the second hand section. Alex watched him, hoping that the dark haired guy would prove to be part of that select clientele that Alex handled better than anyone else. But it was only after the other customers had left the store that the shopper approached the counter.

Alex took him in. His wide shoulders, thick glasses and hazel coloured eyes. He was tall and handsome. But when he opened his mouth to ask about a Joni Mitchell title, Alex snapped him a look of contempt.

"I'm sorry," the customer said, with the hint of an American accent. "Have I disturbed you?"

"No," Alex said primly. "But why on earth would you want that tired old record?"

The customer let out a small snort.

"It's not for me," he said, looking at Alex and smiling. "I scratched my friend's copy, so I need to replace it. She insists on still playing it even though the stylus keeps skipping through *Carey*, which, if you ask me, is the only decent song on the whole album."

Alex smiled at the customer's candour. He stood up and walked out from behind the counter.

"Come this way," Alex said, careful not to swish too hard.

"Lesbians are so protective of Joni Mitchell. It's so predictable," Alex muttered, flicking through the *M* artists.

"She is a bit," the customer conceded with a laugh. "But she's a good friend."

"Who? Joni Mitchell?"

"No. Sarah."

Alex handed the record over and inspected the guy again before returning to the counter. Out of towners weren't worth the effort.

The customer continued to flick through the records, but Alex noticed him watching. When the customer eventually returned to the counter with a slew of 45s and *Blue*, Alex bashed the numbers into the cash register.

"What's your name baby?" Alex asked, handing him a paper bag and the receipt.

"Benjamin Cohen. *Ben.* Yours?"

"I'm *Alekzandr*," he said, popping his gum and smiling.

"Well, it's very nice to meet you Alekzandr."

"Well actually, my friends call me Alex," he confessed, suddenly feeling a fraud.

Seeing Ben smile, Alex smiled cockily, looking Ben over and chewing away at his gum like it was a lifeline.

They stood at the counter chatting uninterrupted for almost half an hour until another customer arrived, the bell on the back of the door signalling an end to their flirting.

"Anyway, I'm here for a few more days," Ben finally said after the other customer was safely in the punk section at the far end of the store.

Alex smiled at Ben.

"Listen, do you have a number that I can call you on?" Ben asked.

"Not really. I mean I'm here from Monday to Friday in the afternoons, but my boss goes mental when I get personal calls."

"Because guys are always calling you?" Ben asked, smiling.

"Ha! No, nothing like that. It's more like my office number."

"For what?" Ben asked.

"I do gigs. I'm a DJ and a dancer."

"I didn't know," Ben said, raising his eyebrows.

"How could you? You're not from here."

Ben looked at Alex strangely for a moment.

"Listen, I'm free tonight if you want to get some dinner and a drink," Ben said, breaking into his smile.

***

Because it was a Tuesday night and they only had thirty–two quid in cash between them, they settled on a curry place for a quick bite and a few pints at an off licence Alex occasionally frequented.

It was Alex's first ever *proper* date, and easily more romantic than the countless number of encounters he'd already had.

And from those inauspicious beginnings in a takeout joint, they became a reasonably frequent couple, together whenever Ben was in town.

Sid Vicious may have died, and it may have rocked some of Alex's circles in London, but Alex was finally in the mood to celebrate, even if everyone around him was grieving.

Ben had done what few others in Alex's wide circle of friends had been able to. He'd breathed fresh air into Alex's life and gave him something to obsess about other than his hand to mouth existence. With time, Ben's motivation and self–determination also rubbed off on Alex. As the months passed and people moved on from Sid's death, Alex began examining his life and goals, propelled by Ben's belief that he could be doing something more productive and rewarding with his time.

And it seemed that Alex finally knew what it was that he wanted to concentrate on. *Music.*

With Ben temporarily back in New York again, Alex found the courage and time to try and piece together bits of the song that had been floating around in his head for months. He did his best to concentrate on the Indian styled melody that played in his head in the mornings and scribbled down verses in the margins of whatever book he was reading.

Sitting down to consciously document his ideas was hard. But he did his best to try and transform them into chords, testing them out on his guitar, and humming and making notes as he went.

When Shelly's boyfriend was around, Alex asked for help, looking for advice on how to identify the music in the chaos of his notes.

It took close to a month, but when Alex finally felt he had the basis of a song to work with, he spent most of his evenings hopping around the city, using his friends' equipment to record its various parts. The guitar was done in a bedsit in Islington, the keyboards and vocals in a spare room in Hackney and a very simple programmed sequence was put together at a kitchen table in Shepherd's Bush.

With Ben stuck in New York, Alex began to plug away at the other song ideas that came to him, constructing them in much the same way, but more rapidly.

When he'd come up with six songs, he began to think about how they could be something more than a memento.

At the record store he racked his brain trying to think of the name of the record producer who often came in. Alex hadn't seen him in months but remembered that the guy had once bragged about having a little studio in East London. The guy seemed to pop up every now and then in the music press in connection to whichever protégé he was working with.

Meanwhile, after a life modelling session on a particularly chilly morning, a conversation with one of the students he knew led Alex to discover that the college had the equipment he needed to finish his demos.

He set about trying to find someone he knew in the music department who he could convince to let him play around with the TEAC 2340. With it, he'd be able to feed all his recordings through the multitrack and produce full, complete demo versions of all his patchwork songs.

***

When the producer finally returned to the store, Alex made a song and dance of it, finally remembering his name was Ryan. Alex handed Ryan an envelope which he said had been expressly left for him by someone on the local club scene who knew Ryan came in regularly.

In a moment of weakness, Ryan accepted the package, chuffed that someone had thought of him. Truth be told, he hadn't had a breakthrough act in ages and was down to considering any kind of gig available for the taking.

Ryan took the songs home and listened to them and initially felt like it had been a waste of time even playing them. They sounded incredibly amateur and aside from some striking melodies there was little he enjoyed in them.

But a few days later he found himself humming one of the tunes and after receiving notice on a bunch of utility bills, he looked at the tape on his desk and decided that perhaps he could give it another chance.

Ryan knew the demo belonged to the store clerk. That nasally voice was unmistakeable. But as part of his research, he asked around and found that Alex was indeed considered a rising star, albeit on a very low rung of the underground circuit.

Although he wasn't prepared to return to the store just yet, when Ryan saw a street press listing for *Vinyl Tiger* at an underground leather club, he decided to head on down despite his doubts.

That night, hugging a rum and coke, Ryan watched Alex's set from a secluded corner of the club, impressed by how Alex seemed to have no problems in mixing old Hindi records by Lata Mangeshkar or Manna Day with his own demos and other songs from street culture. Alex would even step away from the turntables and dance as the songs played, pulling people up onto the stage or diving down to dance with them for a few chaotic minutes. Surprised by the antics, Ryan figured Alex might just have enough crass appeal and oversized personality to suggest some potential after all.

When Ryan did return to the record store it was with a new view of the young hustler.

"You know, it's thanks to you that I visited my first ever gay club the other night."

"Really?" Alex smiled. "Why? Were you looking for me?"

"Yes," Ryan admitted, grimacing at the kid's cockiness. "But not in the way you think. It was research."

"Research for what?"

"To see if you were worth all the fuss you made over yourself when you gave me your tape."

"Oh," Alex replied. Then he beamed. "And I guess you decided I was."

Alex's goal was to mix the bombastic Hindi pop in his head with something electronic. Ryan found the concept ridiculous but given the reaction of the clubbers that night, had to concede there could be a market for it.

"What you're saying is that you basically want me to turn your songs into ethnic disco moments?" Ryan asked.

"Exactly! An exploding ethnic disco!" Alex replied, clapping his hands.

Using four of the songs Alex had written, the two sporadically set to work, typically late at night to leave Ryan free during the day for any corporate jobs.

Alex watched Ryan work, hoping to learn something from Ryan's dexterity with the sequencers and programmers. Because money was so tight, they made an unorthodox but typical arrangement. In return for the studio time and costs, Ryan would be credited as a co–writer of each of the four songs he'd chosen to develop, the song writing royalties to be split in perpetuity.

Ryan insisted on rerecording all the musical parts of the demos, but as neither could afford to pay professional musicians, Alex had to convince two friends from a band he knew to play for him. He bartered a deal to design one record sleeve for the band for each day they worked in the studio. To save money, Ryan also mastered the completed recordings himself. And on returning from New York, Ben shelled out for the cost of the demo tapes which would be sent off to various record labels.

Though the demo tape, its disco sound and Alex's wafer–thin vocals met with all kinds of resistance at record companies around London, having four professionally recorded songs gave Alex's live act a significant push. In the summer of 1979, on the strength of the refined demos, Alex booked his first proper live appearance at a club in West London.

Rehearsing for a week with three of his fellow cage dancers, they came up with choreography for the songs. Some simple props were also co–opted into the act; red chairs and brightly coloured parasols that Alex had found in Chinatown which he hoped would complement the costumes he and a friend were creating from a cheap, garish sari fabric they'd found. Alex also designed and printed off flyers at the art college, which he and his friends then distributed around London, their excitement building.

The idea of performing didn't seem to be bothering Alex. He felt sufficiently rehearsed and instead began to fixate on just how many people the show might attract.

When one a.m. rolled around the night of his performance, Alex was a bundle of nerves but in good spirits. The photos taken before the performance pointed to his first stage incarnation. In them, Alex wore a garish, sleeveless jumpsuit in a fabric that had a mind and ecosystem all its own. His hair was henna red again and slicked back, his caramel eyes glistening behind a wall of kohl, staring out excitedly under the huge *bindi* he'd stuck on his forehead. He was tall and lithe and proudly told anyone and everyone that he was the reincarnation of Ziggy Stardust, by way of Kerala.

Ben had brought his own Polaroid camera along and used up four film packs taking shots of Alex, his mismatched dancers and the regular crew who made up their extended London family.

There were a little over 150 people in the tiny club, mostly distributed around the modest stage. It was perhaps only six or seven square meters in total, but from the moment the lights went down and came back on for the opening strains of *Tiger Stripes*, Alex prowled every inch of it.

The gaudy Hindi sound and the pumping beats got the punters moving, but mostly, they were focused on him and the dancers and on the simple but striking visual impression they made.

Alex used a microphone to sing over his backing tracks and the effect was sometimes jarring and off key. But people couldn't take their eyes off what was happening on stage. And whatever the music lacked seemed to be made up for by Alex's undeniable stage presence.

By the second song, the bulk of his friends who had earlier lined up for a free bump of coke were now commandeering the front part of the audience, dancing vigorously to *Beat* – a play on where gays meet out in the open.

Taking a moment to regroup before launching into the next song, Alex made a dedication to Ben.

"This song is the first song I ever wrote. It's called *When You're Away*, and Ben, wherever you are down there, it's thanks to you."

As Alex sung live against the backing track, the dancers carried out their choreography from the chairs on the stage. Despite wanting to watch Alex, Ben found himself following the dancers' every move as they stretched and contorted in unison, their movements long and languid.

The excitement of finally bringing these songs to life for the first time in a proper club gave Alex a huge adrenaline rush. As he wound up the final verse on *Hand To Mouth,* the deafening applause and cat calls from his friends in the audience made Alex realise the gig was already over. Thrilled that he'd averted any disasters, Alex smiled and began to thank everyone for coming but was soon drowned out by the resident DJ who began playing the latest Blondie track at high volume.

Off stage, the festivities continued until dawn when Alex and Ben finally cabbed it back to Ben's apartment, their cab driver unable to keep a straight face at Alex's messy, smudged stage makeup.

It took Alex nearly ten minutes to remove the warpaint, and the black leggings, bracelets and layers of shredded singlets he'd changed into after the performance. Once he had, he took the £30 that the club had paid him (the dancers had received £10 each) and lodged it within the pages of the Sylvia Plath anthology he was no longer reading.

After luxuriating in his first hot shower in a week he found Ben asleep in bed and lay there watching him until all the adrenaline finally drained itself from his own body.

***

Over the following months Alex managed to get booked at clubs in London and Manchester.

Although the costumes were sometimes changed, the choreography stayed much the same for the shows. Some audiences were as small as 50 or 60 people but occasionally he filled small venues to capacity.

Word had spread around London about Alekzandr and the clubby Kerala music he was making, and as a result, doors at the record labels finally opened to him.

After the head of a tiny independent label attended one of Alex's gigs, he offered Alex a deal to release two singles and Ryan the chance to work with one of the label's recent acquisitions.

Though the label wasn't wild about Alex's demos, they were nonetheless prepared to test the waters. Their only caveat was that the songs be remastered to be more disco friendly. The belief was that although the songs were probably too *exotic* for British audiences, there was a chance they could sell in Europe.

As instructed, Ryan recalibrated the tracks into more standard disco mixes which Alex immediately hated. Hated so much, that on hearing them in Ryan's studio, he exploded into a rage.

Ryan watched as Alex let out his anger, relieved the tantrum was mostly vocal. As Alex exhausted every expletive in the book and made threats against the label staff and Ryan himself – *for being the ultimate traitor* – Ryan looked at him with a sympathy he never thought he'd have for Alex.

"They're just songs kiddo. It always works like this. You have to play their game first. Then, if you survive, you get to play it on your terms. Right now, you mean nothing to them, just like I don't. They're not interested in what you have to say or what you're trying to do. They just see you as a zero. But if you can get them to see you as a series of zeros, like a five figure zero, or a six figure zero, then, suddenly you become somebody for them."

Ryan looked at Alex. They both needed this.

"So be prepared to swallow your pride a little bit. Start thinking about what you want to do next, because right now, we don't even have a 50/50 chance of getting any further than we already have. This is business. Not art. You have to start understanding that. Once you do, you'll have a better chance of succeeding and doing what you actually want."

Tiger Stripes was sent for pressing, with a simple record sleeve that Alex designed. Word of mouth helped it sell around 7,000 copies in the UK, and a similar number across Western Europe. Its success led to *Beat* also being issued as a single, and though it sold about 9,000 copies in the UK it largely bombed across Europe.

Though neither song received airplay in the UK, both made brief appearances on the UK charts, respectively peaking at No.73 and No.71 in the UK Top 75. Seeing his stage name *Vinyl Tiger* listed, albeit at the bottom of the national charts, still felt like success in Alex's eyes. The label however, decided not to pursue any other releases with him even if they added Ryan to their stable of producers, allegedly packing Ryan's schedule so much that he never again found the time to answer or return any of Alex's calls.

Once the singles saga cooled somewhat and Alex performed his last booked gig, Ben found the courage to take him out of London for a weekend to get his mind off things.

"You know I've been looking for something a little more substantial lately, don't you?" Ben said, his voice thick and syrupy as usual.

"Work wise?" Alex asked.

"Yeah. Well, I've been offered a good full–time role. It's pretty well paid and I think it could be fun. It would mean that I'd become the only New York rep for the company."

Alex looked at Ben for a moment and then out towards the water.

"Are we in Brighton because you need to tell me you won't be coming to London anymore?" Alex asked.

"No. And Yes. I mean I won't be coming here every month anymore. But I was thinking… maybe you could come to New York. Seeing how the label thing isn't working here for you anymore."

"That would mean starting over," Alex said, smarting over the label comment.

"Well, not really. You'd have me."

"I don't want to seem rude, but that's not really enough."

"I know what you're saying, but you would do really well there, you know? They'll love you, I know it."

"Sounds a bit *A Star Is Born* to me," Alex replied.

Ben laughed. "Maybe. A little. But seriously. You still have your records; you can at least shop them around even if they're not everything you wanted them to be."

"No I can't. They belong to Ryan and the label. They're not even mine."

"Yeah, but you can tell the labels in New York that you've already sold thousands of records in Europe and the UK. Forget London, New York is where it's at."

"I don't know Ben. I've gotten used to it here. Things are just starting to work out for me, even if they're not."

"Yeah, but I've gotten used to you too."

Alex fidgeted with the dozens of bracelets concealing his wrists.

"I'm not sure. I don't think I have the energy to start over."

"*Lekke*, I can pay for the airfare." Ben said, using his nickname for Alex in an attempt to pre-empt having his head bitten off.

"So can I. If I ever receive my royalties, but it's not about that. It's just, I don't know, it seems kind of crazy to just up and leave because *you* have to."

"Well I don't want you to see it as a punishment. But I'd hate for us to stop seeing each other just because I have to take a job there. Besides, it's New York I'm asking you to come to, not Siberia."

"Can't you find something else? Here?" Alex asked.

"*Lekke* I was lucky to find what I did where I did. It's not the easiest time to find a job."

"And yet you'd have me move continent," Alex said.

"Yeah, but I'll help you out. I have an old rental apartment in Brooklyn my parents gave me. It's small, but you could take it."

"Where would you be?" Alex asked, combing his hand through the sand.

"In Manhattan, sharing," Ben said dismissively. "I don't see what you have to lose though. Come over, give it a couple of months and if you don't like it, you can just come back to London."

"Wait, you would have me move countries, but you won't live with me?"

"You're a free spirit Alex. You need your own time, your own space."

"But I want to see you all the time."

"No, you don't," Ben snorted.

"No, you're right," Alex responded, laughing and relieved that the tone had lightened. "I just wanted to see how that sounded."

"Listen, think about it at least. London will always be here. But I'll be there, making sure you enjoy it. And if you sort things out with a label here, then it's only a flight back. You're not moving back to Australia, for god's sake."

Indeed, the consensus among Alex's friends was that he was a fool to want to hang around London when New York was on offer. London, they constantly reminded him, had gone to the dogs.

"Plus, Ben's a keeper," Shelly reminded him from the kitchen beanbag. "You'd be mad to throw him and the Big Apple away like that."

She looked at him and seemed to hesitate. But then she spoke.

"And let's face it. A catch like Ben will be snapped up in no time. And where's that going to leave you? Doing your gigolo thing in the clubs? Come on."

"Are you just saying all of this stuff so that your boyfriend can move in?"

"No. I'm saying all this because you're better than all that Alex. And Ben's the only one that's made you see it."

| **4** |

BROOKLYN

The royalties were lower than Alex had hoped for, but he still had to fight tooth and nail for them. It was the most money he'd seen since leaving Tokyo and with it, he bought himself a one way ticket to NYC, shipping his meagre belongings to the Brooklyn address Ben had given him.

In the week leading up to his flight, Alex's nerves began to get the better of him, they only beginning to dissipate once he completed customs at JFK.

"There's that smell of Yatagan I missed," Alex said, taking in Ben's cologne as Ben warmly hugged him outside arrivals, helping Alex with some of his improvised carry on bags.

Ben drove him all the way to the Brooklyn apartment while Alex, all wide eyed, took in the panorama of buildings that seemed like debutantes draped in smog.

The apartment wasn't quite what he expected. He had imagined a handsome brownstone but instead found a 1960s brick building with no elevator. Tiny and a little dusty, it couldn't have been any more than 30 square metres in size, but Ben told him that the fire escape also doubled as an unofficial balcony. Though it was spartanly furnished, Ben had changed the sheets and seen to the utilities.

They fucked and straight afterwards went for a walk around the borough, Alex keen to take in his new surroundings. *God damn New York City.* Well, Brooklyn at least.

Ben pointed out the staples of the area; the local Korean, which would become Alex's morning temple for cigarettes and whatever fruit was on offer, and some of the cheap eat places that he used to go to when he lived in the area.

Within a week Alex was pounding the pavement. He quickly found some viciously underpaid waiting work and, through one of Ben's acquaintances, a reasonably regular gig as a backing vocalist.

In addition to accepting almost any work on offer, Alex made it his mission in his first six months to meet and befriend as many people as he could, desperate to forge a life similar to the one he had in London.

By night he hit the downtown scene hard, sometimes with Ben, but mostly without. Telling anyone he met that he was a European dance act helped him connect with all kinds of people, but he quickly managed to forge two friendships without relying on his credentials. One was with Jasper, a final year film student and bus boy who often snuck Alex into the club he worked at, the other, with Ian, a Kiwi who was a courier by day, a waiter by night and an aspiring songwriter/musician to boot.

Using the contacts he made through his backing vocal work, Alex wrangled a few bookings across the metropolitan area for his uniquely chaotic DJing gigs. It wasn't long before many of the venues invited him to return with his full act and it took little effort to convince Jasper and Miles, another new addition to his social circle, to act as his backup dancers once he dusted off his old routines and the costumes which had finally arrived from the UK.

Though he had no phone of his own, he went to great lengths to make himself available to venue managers, ever fearful his supervisors at the restaurants would pull him up for treating their phone lines as his own personal answering service.

Ben seemed to split his week between Manhattan and Brooklyn. When letting himself into the apartment, Ben would, without fail apologize, promising he had every intention of telling his Manhattan flatmate that he was gay.

For a long time, Alex chose not to press Ben for further details. Though he mostly tolerated their split arrangement, his late nights downtown would've been easier if Ben could've agreed to sleep overs in Manhattan.

In any case, Alex found that between his commitments to his recently revived career, his long nights downtown and his erratic working schedule, the little time he had to spend with Ben was a welcome distraction.

For someone who was officially a living unemployment statistic, Alex's schedule was hectic. Any free time not already accounted for was spent loitering in New York's Music Building, where he occasionally did some backup vocals for a range of groups.

He did his best to concentrate on the part of his life in New York that was teaming with possibilities, not the one with Ben which seemed constrained and curtailed. But if he was honest, it wasn't just the flatmate situation that bugged him. Overall, Ben seemed less invested in him here than he had been in London. It was true, Ben had introduced Alex to a couple of older gay friends, but beyond that, most of Ben's personal life still remained off limits to Alex, and Alex wasn't sure why. He oscillated between the idea that Ben was simply giving him his space and the dread that Ben was hiding something. He didn't know which of his instincts to follow. But curiosity sometimes got the better of him, and, on one late night after performing at a seedy downtown club, Alex insisted they sleep at the Manhattan apartment.

At first Ben offered to pay for a cab back to Brooklyn but it quickly became clear that Alex wasn't going to budge.

"I don't see what the problem is. I can even sleep on the sofa if your roomie is home. I'll scrape off all this make up and play hetero before I even get into the cab."

"It's not you," Ben sighed.

"What is it then? Ben I've been here almost a year now. I still don't know where you live. That doesn't strike you as strange? Plus, I don't want to go back to Brooklyn tonight."

"*Lekke,* I wish you would just trust me."

"I have. All this time. But it's eating away at me. You're hiding something. And I know you don't live with your parents. You told me they live in Florida. It's not that, right?"

"No, it's not that."

A gust of wind sent Alex's felt hat scurrying down the footpath. The two of them had to chase it repeatedly as the bursts of air sent it hurtling every time one of them got close.

"Maybe it is easier if I do just take you home," Ben said, finally securing the runaway hat and putting it on. "Then you can see for yourself."

"Oh, I hate it when you're cryptic. Why don't you save us both the shitshow and just tell me now."

"No, it's best if you do actually see where I live. Come on."

Alex reluctantly followed Ben into a cab that zipped them out to Two Bridges, which Ben flatly explained was where his parents had bought him an apartment a few years earlier, before they left the city.

The lift took them to the fifth floor of a reasonably pristine building and Ben led Alex down an anodyne corridor to the furthermost door, marked 504.

Alex suddenly felt self-conscious. It was one thing to be dressed this way on stage, but quite another in a place that clearly had a co-op.

Ben opened the door to reveal a spacious apartment tastefully decorated with contemporary furnishings. There were a few paintings and framed prints on the wall and the lighting was soft and homey. Alex took in the open plan room with the same wonderment he'd reserved for New York's skyline. As he clocked the room, a photo frame on a far lampstand caught his eye. He put his silver bag down on the rug and then slowly walked across the room, his bracelets jingling as he approached the lampstand.

Ben closed and deadlocked the door behind them, watching Alex prowl across the room. He could see Alex was headed straight to the black and white photo and without a word, he sat on the sofa and braced himself.

Alex's instinct was to tear Ben apart when he saw the photo up close. Looking at it, he hated himself and hated his instincts even more. Brooklyn had been exhausting at times, but Manhattan, it turns out, was humiliating.

"She's really pretty," Alex finally said. "Where is she?"

"Tel Aviv. Well actually, I think she's in Haifa at the moment."

Alex wanted to scream. Instead he probed further.

"She there on holiday?"

"Not really," Ben said, squirming on the pleather sofa.

"You both look pretty young."

"I was twenty three. Pretty much the same age you are now. It was arranged by our parents."

"The photo?" Alex quipped, bringing it over to the sofa.

"The marriage," Ben said, sternly.

"Yes of course. So, what, was it twelve years ago?"

"Close enough to fourteen actually," Ben said.

Alex sat down next to him and watched coldly as Ben's eyes watered.

"Were you seeing each other or was it a blind arrangement? Like, because you never brought girls home?"

"Something like that. The second option," Ben confessed, wiping a tear from his eye.

"I see. I don't see any pictures of any kids."

"We don't have any. It's not that kind of relationship."

"You mean you don't sleep together?" Alex asked.

"No. Never. Well, twice. To consecrate it, I guess. Once on the wedding night and once on the honeymoon."

"I see. But I don't see why you didn't just tell me from the start."

"Come with me," Ben said, motioning for Alex to follow him.

Alex wasn't sure he wanted to explore the hell he was in any further, but Ben led him into a corridor, turning on the light in an adjoining room. It was a bedroom, swathed in pastel pinks and peaches. He then turned on the light in the adjacent room, revealing another bedroom with another double bed, this time decked out in blue and white.

"Pink and blue," Alex noted. "Your taste or hers?"

"I didn't bring you here for a lesson on interior design. I brought you here because you need to see things with your own eyes. Not just hear the parts you want to, tuning out the rest like you always do."

Alex dropped his head.

"Be as flippant about things as you want. You can. You have that luxury. I don't," Ben said. "We made a vow to each other. To respect each other. She doesn't ask me any questions, and I don't ask her any. And neither of us thinks our own needs are more important than the other's."

"What kind of way is that to live Ben?"

"It's the kind of way you live when you don't want to hurt somebody. You're not the only one that makes sacrifices Alex. She gave up her job last year to be in Israel with her family. She's looking after both of her parents. Doesn't know when she'll be back in New York. Doesn't know when she'll be able to be with her friends again. To do the job she loves or enjoy being in the city she adores."

Alex had learned to hate married men for the most part. He usually found them sanctimonious, always capable of justifying their behaviour, as if their desires were more important than anyone else's.

In his experience, married men were as happy to justify a lack of interest in their spouses as they were willing to throw a little cash at him or someone like him. It was as if it was safe for them to pursue people like him who seemed to be living for the moment. But only from the comfort of a life they could always fall back on.

Alex thought he'd become an expert at steering clear of them, even if they'd infiltrated his stomping grounds. He could usually spot them a mile away because it was easy to identify the men obsessed with elaborate worlds of smoke and mirrors. The men who thought they were so good at camouflaging what they really felt and what they needed people like Alex to do for them.

Alex sat at the edge of Ben's bed and finally looked at him as Ben spoke.

"I know we'll separate eventually. I don't know when exactly but we have talked about it. Probably after her parents pass. But not yet."

Ben joined Alex on the bed.

"I didn't want you to come here. I wanted to spare you all of this. But I didn't want you thinking I just want to keep you on the side or that I'm going to promise to leave her for you and not come through. I thought about being ballsy like you once, I really did. Even thought about disappearing. To the east coast. But

I guess my family's approval was more important to me in the end. I never thought my life would turn out like this, it's not at all what it's cracked up to be. It's exhausting, you know?"

Although Alex was listening, his mind was busy plotting how to raze everything and everyone in the city. It wasn't just Ben he wanted to hurt. Part of him was glad that Ben was unravelling, bleeding out more truths now than he ever had in their two years together. But he hated the fact that, even then, Ben still had the upper hand, lies or not.

After years of constantly pushing, ignoring any resistance just to carve out a space for himself, Alex was often incapable of realising how precarious his position in the world really was.

But in that moment, he finally saw it. Saw how Ben had made New York happen for him. Had a roof over his head and some simple creature comforts because of Ben. And yet prior to barging into Ben's comfortable, clean, organized apartment, Ben had never once made him feel like a tramp. Never treated him like the bejewelled, kohled sidepiece he saw himself as. The kind of person who knew full well they did not belong in a place like this.

"I think I should just go," Alex said, getting up. "I can't believe you let me come up like this. Where's the bathroom? I need to wash all this shit off," Alex said, desperately clawing at his own face. "What if someone in the building saw me? They're gonna think you've got a thing for trade," he said, his breathing accelerating, "where's the bathroom?" he panted, his nails drawing blood from his cheeks.

"Alex, stop it!" Ben said, grabbing his wrists and pulling them down by his sides. "Stop it! Breathe! You're not going anywhere.

I want you to stay. We'll sleep on it, and tomorrow we'll talk it through. I didn't bring you here to end things Alex. I've opened the door to all of this because you're important to me," Ben said, struggling to keep Alex still.

"Let me go, I have to leave," Alex yelled, desperate for air.

"Stop it!" Ben screamed, "Alex stop it! Don't do this, goddammit!"

And just then, Ben did something to Alex that no one had done in years.

He broke his heart.

Not by trying to humiliate him or by threatening to leave him. He did it by showing Alex compassion. In doing so, he made Alex feel awful for pushing and pushing all the time. For never giving Ben the credit he deserved.

And Alex dropped to the floor, crying for the first time in years, the tears gushing out from the cracks in his heart and dripping down from his eyes. Once they'd started, he was powerless to stop them. Ben simply sat on the floor next to him, holding him and whispering encouraging apologies.

When the tears finally stopped flowing, Alex looked for the courage to look past his clumpy eyelashes and up at Ben. Doing so, he realised Ben was a *different* kind of married man. One who was more than just smoke or mirrors.

"Come on," Ben said, holding out his hand, "Let's get you freshened up. I don't want all that shitty mascara on my pillows."

| 5 |

BURST

"Burst was such an on–off album. We started working on the songs in 1981 right after Alekzandr won his contract, but he got dropped by his label soon after," recalled Ian Smith, one of Alex's besties and the album's main co–writer.

"When he eventually got another deal in 1982, the new label wasn't so crash hot on us recording an entire album. They wanted to limit things to a couple of singles," Ian explained.

"There was a lot of upheaval in the disco divisions. A lot of artists were getting signed but then being given the boot the minute there was a reshuffle."

"I never got the feeling Alekzandr was really secure at the second label. But they gave him $4,000 for some publishing rights, so he decided we should use a good chunk of it on some studio time. Because the label was umming and ahhing about finding him a producer, we figured we'd do it ourselves."

Ian was recounting the events to a music journalist, who years later, was reassessing the impact that a slew of dance acts had on early eighties pop.

"It was a baptism of fire learning how to do stuff in the studio with limited time and resources. I think Alex would've preferred someone at the label to just green light us and have someone with experience show us the ropes.

"But he just put his head down and focused. We had four or five really good songs in the can. And we were resourceful. And Jasper, who was graduating from film school, had the genius idea of using the money to film a couple of music videos. Alex was consistently gigging downtown and in New Jersey and he already had a loyal following. People were really into Alex's gigs because they were really presentational. So Jasper convinced him that a couple of music videos would sure up his place at the label.

"We piled into a couple of cars and headed down to Montauk. Jasper wanted videos that had a bit of a surfy vibe to them and Montauk was the closest place we could think of even though it was nearly winter. They were kind of bonfire and surf videos with some terrible dancing that we thought was cool at the time, but they seemed to sum up our vibe. We were this weird collective of arty kids who were mixing things up and there wasn't anyone else like us. Plus, Alekzandr had that amazing look he has, so Jasper managed to come up with some great footage.

"It was a risk using the money like that, but when we got back to New York, Jasper edited the footage and we realised we had something. Alekzandr didn't have a manager so he asked me to go with him to the label offices for some moral support. He had a plan."

After waiting almost an hour in the label's reception area, Alex and Ian were ushered into a tiny meeting room.

"Alekzandr, the timing is just not right," the rep said, apologetically. "Right now the focus should be on your shows here in the tri state area. Once you get some traction, we can push things a little. But we can't green light your record just yet."

"I don't need you to green light my record," Alex said, the rep looking at him confused. "I just need you to write something on a letterhead for me."

"But you've already got a contract," the A&R guy said, cocking his head.

"I'm not asking you to make me a deal. I'm asking you to do some clerical work," Alex explained, Ian watching on, impressed.

"I want you to get a letterhead and simply type out 'for your consideration' and then I want you to stamp it or sign it or do whatever you do to make it look official."

The A&R guy laughed. "And what are you going to do with it?"

"Your job. I'm going to get the traction you're supposed to create for me. And your bosses are going to kiss your arse once I'm done."

The A&R guy tossed up the idea of doing the kid a favour. It wasn't an unreasonable request and he couldn't see any potential fallout. So he smiled at Alex and asked the boys to follow him to his office.

"Ellen," the rep said, arriving at the secretarial desk. "I need five complimentary notes on letterhead."

"Sure thing," Ellen said, pulling out the leaves from her locked filing cabinet. "How you doing Alekzandr?"

"I'm doing great Ellen, you?"

She typed up the notes, had the rep sign them, and stamped them with the label's rubber stamp.

"Here you go kid," the rep said, handing them over in a manilla folder. "Do your worst."

The following night Alex and Ian met up with Miles, Alex's sometime backing dancer.

"You sure she's okay with doing it?" Alex asked Miles.

"Positive. Made a whole song and dance about how she saw your show and how much they'd love you. Her supervisor told her to bring your stuff in if she thinks it's cool. I think they're testing her to see if she's got the mettle to work there," Miles said.

"How long have you been dating her?" Ian asked.

"We're not dating. We just fuck when her boyfriend is out of town."

Miles' sometime girlfriend came through just as she promised. True to her word, she'd sat with her supervisor, an MTV producer, and explained how Alekzandr was one of the hottest names on the downtown scene.

Within a month, MTV was airing one of the videos, *I Love You*, on light rotation and soon after, DJs for clubs up and down the East coast started requesting copies from the label.

By the time the label sent the song for commercial pressing, Alex had done gigs in Philadelphia, Miami and Boston and *I Love*

You was receiving play in clubs nationwide. MTV moved the song into high rotation and, when it finally reached radio, it entered the lower end of the national charts.

"After a gig in Boston, we were summoned to the label offices," Ian explained. "By gosh you should've seen how different the A&R guy's tone was. The head of the division was with him, and they told Alex he needed to get into the studio right away to work on an album. Because things were so rushed, they told us that all our demos would end up on the album. It was a dream scenario for us."

As the boys entered the studio, paired with a New York producer to complete the tracks, *I Love You* went into its second pressing, and began its long, steady climb in the top forty in April 1983. As it rose in the top forty, MTV also began to air Jasper's other video, *Smash*.

When *I Love You* entered the top twenty, the promotional demands began to eat into Alex's studio time. In between sessions, the label hastily organised photo shoots in makeshift studios and on the Lower East Side streets to service to the press. The label also prepared a press bio – full of errors –describing *Alekzandr* as a New York club kid with a bent for the outdoors. It explained he was a new acquisition who had already achieved success across the pond; an artist who was finally breaking out of the underground scene.

Some at the label worried that Alekzandr's style was a little too risqué for audiences. One label publicist privately told a journalist at the time, "I don't have any idea what to do with him. He's not exactly Boy George or Marilyn but he's no Nik Kershaw or Howard Jones either. He looks like he smells, you know. Just, unmarketable and yet poppy at the same time."

The reality was that Alekzandr could have been any one of the faceless one hit wonders on the club circuit had he not broken through via MTV.

With pressure mounting to complete his album, the idea of having to sit through his first ever interviews proved another source of anxiety for Alex. He had no idea of what he was expected to say and no plan on how much to disclose about his life. But in order to play catch up, his label put him to work on the phone and in grungy coffee shops across New York, where he talked to the music press.

Alex spent a week agonising the minute he was told his first ever interview had been booked for him. Jasper had told him that a good pop star knows when to embellish and when to spin even the darkest of events, but Alex didn't know where to start in recounting his last five years.

But when he realised little was required of him other than to answer the most tedious of questions, Alex's nerves calmed. By the fifth or sixth interview, Alex began to relax and appreciated the candour of one music journalist in particular, who explained things were always awkward when their subjects didn't yet have an LP out. And because Alex fit into that category, the interviewer asked permission to ask some unconventional questions which eventually wound up in an irreverent teen mag.

"Alekzandr, what are three things people should know about you?"

"I need to have some more fun, not that this isn't fun, but I'm working a lot right now so I'm itching to get up to some mischief.

"I grew up in a Christian house but I ran away to an ashram in India, so my beliefs are a bit mixed up. And, um, this morning was the first morning I didn't skip breakfast this week. I pulled an all nighter with a friend of mine and by day he works at a coffee shop near my recording studio. So he invited me in for a free feed when he saw me walking past."

"Your song is called I Love You. How many times have you said it? And how many times have you meant it?"

"Gosh, I probably say it about ten times a day. I say it to my friends and sometimes I say it to random strangers. Like last week on the subway someone recited a poem to me, so I told them that I loved them.

"Romantically I don't have any problems saying it. I don't count the number of people I say it to but, when I say it, I always mean it, even if it means something different to me than it does to other people."

"What's on the horizon for you?"

"I'm just finishing up my debut album, which I hope will be released soon. In the meantime, I've got some club shows to prepare for, so more rehearsals for them, and, you know… just hanging out in New York. Same as always."

"Finally, can you tell us what that is on your forehead?"

"It's a bindi. A third eye. I like to believe it protects me from people's bad energy. It's kind of like a crucifix but you wear it on your face."

***

Smash entered the top forty the week Alex began work on two final tracks for the album which were proving problematic.

To meet the deadlines, the label had sourced the songs from external writers, in part also to bolster Alex and Ian's songs.

While much of the recording process had to be rushed, Allen Black, the album's producer, had taken the time to modify some of the boys' tracks, which added a layer of tension to the recording process. The boys were furious that Black stripped some of their songs of the quirks they had built into them, but this time it was Alex that warned Ian not to make a fuss.

"Don't fight him on it. Trust me. I've been down that road before. It doesn't get you anywhere."

In an interview years later, Black recalled the moment when he told Alex it was the label that had made him make the changes.

"Alekzandr really took it to heart. Couldn't understand why I was picking apart his and Ian's work. In a way he was very precocious at the time and working with him in the studio was tough sometimes, especially towards the end, because I knew I was undoing a lot of their hard work," Black recalled.

"But I kept warning Alekzandr that he needed more live instruments in the mix. That without them the music would date really quickly. That's why I brought in the guitars and some more drums."

"At first he was furious, but then he made me talk through my work step by step. He said I'd betrayed him and Ian, and that to make up for it, I had to show him the ropes. Honestly, it was really tense at times, because while I was criticising him, his songs were blowing up in the charts. I was second guessing myself at one point because his music was suddenly everywhere.

"In the end, he had some input into the changes. He didn't know what he was talking about on a technical level, but by god, he already had an ear for things. Even way back then."

***

Emerging from the studio with a completed debut album, four years after recording his first song, Alex finally secured himself the services of a manager.

Michael Estes, an A&R guy from his previous American label had contacted him, explaining that he too had been hung out to dry in the label's latest reshuffle.

"You're so close to getting into the main league," Estes said over a Chinese meal in Brooklyn. "But you're going to need someone who knows how to take you to the next level."

"And what do you know about managing someone? Aren't you in A&R?" Alex said, noisily sucking his noodles into his mouth.

"I know that your label's in damage control mode with you. They can't keep up with demand. And that you've signed things you shouldn't have. You need someone who understands how labels work."

"I think I need someone who can see the bigger picture."

"Oh, that's me, alright," Estes said. "But you also need someone who can get you a better deal than the one you've already agreed to. Someone who knows how to play the label without hurting anyone's feelings. Nobody knows how better than me."

***

As promised, Estes quickly took control of the fate of his new and only client, who now had a third top forty hit in the chart.

Estes set up a series of meetings for Alex with an accounting firm in Brooklyn and a Manhattan based legal studio, to help Alex understand his financial and legal obligations. He also organised for some PR training with a media specialist to prepare Alex for the promotional juggernaut that was just around the corner.

In July 1983, the label finally issued the album, *Burst*, just as the third single *Kiss Me* shot into the US top ten. With that, the public's interest in Alex skyrocketed, a barrage of interviews and reviews for his debut record appearing in the US press.

By the end of the summer of 1983, *Burst* and its singles were already charting in five continents, the singles often competing with one another in the charts. In a bid to get things under control, Estes had the US label postpone the release of the album's next single to October. This was to give the labels in other markets a chance to play catch up and prolong the album's shelf life.

Estes absolutely championed Alex, steering him through the demands the international affiliates and the foreign press made on him, the year's new pop sensation.

At first Estes worked out of his own apartment but was forced to rent an office in Manhattan and take on staff to cope with the workload.

He cherry picked Alex's media appearances throughout the territories, doing his best to avoid overexposure, desperate to avoid Alekzandr being regarded a flash in the pan due to too much intense media interest.

As it was, Alekzandr divided people. Most respectable critics upheld the "singing himbo" moniker an LA-based critic had coined, while only a select few suggested Alekzandr had the makings of a new, important talent. For all his chutzpah, ability to charm, and street smarts, Alex's unconventional persona also worked against him, ruffling the media's feathers as it did.

Estes though, was convinced he had to focus on undoing many of the business mistakes the label had initially made with Alex, and that he needed to strengthen Alex's overall negotiating position now that he had a multimillion selling debut.

On the label's dime, the two of them, along with Jasper and Miles, travelled to ten different countries in the space of six weeks, on a media junket to introduce Alex to audiences beyond the US.

A three week promotional tour in the UK and Europe boasted almost daily television and radio appearances, the promotion coinciding with the official launch of the fourth single, *Without You.*

By the time the crew reached Japan, *Without You* was on its way to becoming a global hit and *Burst* was close to having sold four million copies.

In business meetings, Alex let Michael do all the talking. He watched and listened intently. When the meetings were done, he asked Michael questions. Despite the crushing demands of the schedule, Alex made it his priority to observe and learn; whether in boardrooms, television studios, or at in–store appearances.

After years of struggle, being feted on a daily basis as a 'hot new artist' felt like vindication for all his efforts over the years. And though each day he felt more and more in control of his work, and was learning to implicitly trust Michael, he had no inkling of the mini dramas that awaited them both in Australia.

| 6 |

MELBOURNE

On their final morning in Tokyo, Michael had woken to find Alex quietly sobbing in bed.

"Hey? What's wrong?" Michael asked, opening the curtains slightly and then moving over to the bed, putting his hand on Alex's shoulder.

"Nothing," Alex replied, trying to rub the tears from his eyes.

Michael took a long look at him and then hopped onto the bed, lying next to him.

"It's a day off today. Maybe we've just been working you too much. We're flying out tonight. Today's all about relaxing."

"I know," Alex mumbled, swallowing with difficulty.

Michael lay watching him, thinking about what had happened the night before. Nothing. They'd all danced like mad men until they made their way back to the hotel, their driver visibly relieved that he could call it a night.

Michael thought about what the day had in store; a sightseeing tour organised by Alex's Japanese label representative and a traditional lunch. Some downtime in the city if they wanted it. And then the redeye to Australia.

Australia. And with that, it clicked.

"Oh. Alex, it's going to be fine. You're just nervous. Your family are going to be so happy to see you."

Alex rolled over and faced the door. Michael watched as his body convulsed with its sobbing.

"They're going to be over the moon to see you. And when they see what you've accomplished, if they haven't already, they'll be stoked for you. And, more importantly, you're going to have time to spend with them. And you'll be able to go back and see them again in the new year again and spend even more time with them. You have to think of it like the start of a new period with them, and the end of this period where you just weren't able to see them. Everything will feel normal within half an hour with them. Trust me, families are all the same. You'll be over them in a flash. Happens to me every time I go back to Puerto Rico," Michael said, chuckling at the thought.

"You end up arguing like always over the *funche.* Come on, get up, get dressed. Pack your things. We've got a day ahead to enjoy and things to do to keep your mind busy."

On the plane, Alex watched with frustration as one by one his entourage fell asleep around him while he couldn't sleep a wink.

His mind raced as it rationalised his thoughts, knowing they needed to be in good order for the inevitable family inquisition that awaited him. The notion that moments from his past could sprout back to life after he'd buried them so deeply filled Alex with terror.

It wasn't that he was ashamed of the things he'd done. He just had no confidence that his family would be able to understand his past or the demands that desperation imposes on people.

He'd had time to process things, to work through them a little. But it was only now that his own perception was finally changing. Until recently, he'd viewed his own body as a part of his arsenal that could be deployed to achieve his goals and there were times when others were glaringly aware of it.

Like the time back in 1980 when a record label rep came to one of his New Jersey shows, promising Alex the world if he was prepared to first do him one quick favour. The rep had even helpfully unzipped, proudly unfurling his equipment as if it was a banner. But after briefly contemplating doing what he'd been asked, Alex decided he couldn't. That he couldn't land a contract that way. The rep ridiculed him for freezing up like that, warning Alex that his career would be over before it started if he said anything.

Alex worried that his time in Australia would be swallowed up by all the editing thoughts like that would require. He'd have to steer clear of the anecdotes he freely shared with his friends. Like the ones of waking up covered in cockroaches in his last apartment or having had to share a room with four others in another when things went sour with Ben.

Wouldn't even be able to mention Ben without bringing on an interrogation. Would have to lie, saying he'd lost his grandfather's silver bracelet when the truth was it had disappeared in one of the countless times his apartments had been burgled.

The reckoning that awaited daunted Alex so much that he considered asking Michael to cancel the Melbourne leg of their trip. It seemed so unfair that after finally reaching a time in his life where people were telling him he was worthy, he was back to feeling the opposite.

He'd had to work so hard at rebuilding his life when things with Ben collapsed. Felt like a piece of shit when Ben's wife delivered her own reckoning after a neighbour had reported Alex's sleepovers in her absence. Probably the same neighbour that had once called Alex *scum* on his way out of the lift one morning.

He'd had to watch helplessly as Ben's confidence unravelled in the face of his wife's fury. To listen, horrified, as Ben told him both families had gotten involved and that the initial meetings with a divorce lawyer suggested Ben would be stripped of his home and other assets.

He'd promised to stick by Ben through it all but was bereft when Ben turned to him and told him that he, Alex, was responsible for it all and that things between them were over. Couldn't have known that he wouldn't see or hear from Ben again until 1988, when his management suddenly begun fielding calls on Ben's behalf, long after Alex had buried everything they'd experienced together.

Once the plane entered Australian airspace, Alex decided what one thing he would talk openly about with his family.

Them.

And with that, some of his anxiety lifted and the idea of getting some sleep finally seemed feasible.

***

After checking into their hotel in Sydney, Michael accompanied Alex in the afternoon to the record label offices.

The label's full brass had been assembled, keen, Alex imagined, to make a good first impression.

The head of the local marketing department shared the news that *Without You* had, according to the fax in his hand, officially become a top ten hit in some European territories and in Australia.

Alex beamed at Michael, letting the subsequent explanation of the current local marketing campaign wash over him for a moment until the head of the label interrupted the presentation, explaining he had some pressing news.

"Last night we were informed that the British courts ruled in favour of Alekzandr's original British label. Our injunction was denied."

"Those arseholes. They're just doing it to cash in," Alex said.

"The thinking in our UK office is your old label will rush release all your old songs to take advantage of your current appeal. That means many of the affiliates have decided to hold back on your next single. Maybe permanently."

"Does that affect us?" Alex asked Michael quietly.

"It just means," Michael said, loud enough for everyone in the room to hear, "that we run a bit of a risk of your music saturating the market. When that kind of thing happens it can go in two ways. If you have really fervent fans they'll lap it up. But usually, having so many songs out at one time only turns the wider public off you more quickly. When those songs come out, there's a chance that you'll have five or six singles in record stores competing for people's money."

"And can't we pull some of our own out of the shops now?"

"You don't want to do that Alekzandr," the label head said. "The old ones don't have anything other than your name to sell them. No videos, no specific promotion. They'll be more like collectables if we just let them run their course. Your other songs still have a lot of wind in them. You've got three in the top 40 here just this week."

After dismissing the middle managers, the label head stayed on with Alex and Michael.

"Alekzandr let me be frank with you. There's a lot of panic in our other offices. Most of them think we all should kill the rest of the campaign for your album and let you ride out the buzz a bit. They're worried all of this will hurt your next album.

"It might seem like a spanner in the works, but if you ask me it's a blessing these songs are coming out. The attention will get you closer to the front of the pack. A step closer to being in Simon Le Bon or Boy George's league.

"You know, some people at the label don't know what to do with you because they think you're a bit too off the wall. You've got to get ready for an even bigger magnifying glass that'll come down on you. You've got Michael, which is good, because he knows how things work, but you'll both have to quickly work out who you can trust. In a network like ours, a lot of new acts get sucked up by the competing ideas and agendas. You've got to play ball."

"Okay," Alex uttered, not knowing what else to say. "Thank you, I guess."

***

His three days in Sydney were mostly packed with interviews for the printed media. He sat in his label's boardroom for almost back to back sessions with journalists from Australia and New Zealand, doing his best to satisfy the local angle of their questions. He lost track of how many times he was asked whether he still considered himself an Aussie and whether there were any specific Aussie artists who had inspired him growing up. He had no trouble answering the former, but when it came to the latter he had to deflect, instead pointing out his love for contemporaries like INXS.

Although he was only rarely asked meatier questions it was a relief just to hear the accent and be in the company of people who seemed genuinely interested in connecting as fellow countrymen.

On his penultimate night in Sydney, along with Jasper and Miles, he performed his showcase gig at *Selina's* for the press and members of the industry, and then again for the public the following night with a sold out show.

Arriving in Melbourne, there was more business to attend to at the record label office. There, Alex spent a couple of hours poring over the notes for his scheduled television appearances and posing for photos with the staff before he and Michael hailed a cab.

With two free days at his disposal, he stayed on in the taxi after it dropped Michael at the hotel.

"Take the long way," Alex told the driver. "I'm not in a hurry."

Driving through Melbourne's north, it looked much like he remembered it. Clean, suburban… drab.

The taxi stopped in the driveway and Alex took his overnight bags out of the trunk himself. He rang the doorbell as he no longer had the keys to the house. They were probably somewhere in India or England now.

He'd swept his hair back into a neat ponytail and was looking a little less edgy than usual in a simple jeans and top ensemble. The door opened and revealed his father, Oliviero, a little portlier, greyer and happier than Alex remembered him looking.

"Alex," Oliviero said, fumbling over the lock on the security door and practically pouncing onto his son. They both needed a moment to compose themselves afterwards, Oliviero holding the screen door open and ushering Alex inside.

"Your mum's on her way home. She was at your aunt's. Your hair's so long!"

"Yeah, has been for a few years now," Alex said, cautiously walking through the hallway.

"You look well."

"I'm sure I look ridiculous."

"All you young people look ridiculous, but you, you look good. Maybe a little tired."

"I had a show last night. Had trouble getting to sleep afterwards."

"I don't think your mum slept a wink either. She had the day off today and was fretting so much I made her leave the house."

"And Sofia? Domenic?"

"They're at work. They're coming for dinner. I think Patrick, Sofia's husband is coming too, but I don't know about Jennifer. You know she's pregnant, no?"

"Jennifer's pregnant? When's the baby due?"

"Oh, next year," Oliviero said, clearly disappointed. "But she's got the morning sickness, so she said she'd see how she feels. But Domenic will definitely come."

"Great," Alex muttered. "What are they like? Patrick and Jennifer?"

"Well, I'm surprised that you didn't come to the weddings. We would've found the money for the tickets somehow."

"Oh I know. Domenic got married right when I was moving to New York, so it was just bad timing. And Sofia when I was in the studio. Anyway, you didn't answer my question."

"Well. Patrick is okay. A bit boring. After all these years he still goes on about the food here. *'Fantastic'. 'Amazing'. 'Oh My Goodness'.* But he's a good man. And Jennifer's the boss, but she's nice. I like her."

"Does mum like them?"

"She likes Patrick but doesn't like Jennifer. And you? Any news?"

"You mean am I getting married?"

"Yes. Tell me now so I can have the heart attack here."

"No. No chance of it."

"You were always different to those two. I remember you in the car with me one day. You were only twelve or thirteen and I was trying to find out if you had a girlfriend. And then you said something like, 'Dad, I'm never going to get married.' You said it like you really meant it."

Alex knew he should say something in response, but he instead pulled out a chair at the table.

"Anyway, I want to know your news. We've been reading a lot about you lately. Seeing you on the television."

"Oh, don't believe half the things they say," Alex said, taking off his shoes and tucking his feet under his thighs. "I wouldn't know how to explain everything."

"You'll tell me when you're ready, I'm sure."

"The most important thing is that you know I have some great friends, my work is finally going well, and the other stuff, well, I'm working that out as I go."

"I have no doubt. I love all three of you. But I knew you'd be the one that had the hardest road," Oliviero said, taking a seat at the table. "Your mum doesn't understand you the way I do," Oliviero said, "she's just a bit more black and white," he added.

Alex shifted on his chair and wanted to bring up another subject.

"I wasn't always your dad, you know. I was young once too. I did things."

"I'm sure you did," Alex said, startled by his father's tone.

"I read what they say about you. Listen to what they're saying. At work everyone was so excited for me in the beginning, to have a famous son."

"I don't think I'm famous dad."

"Of course you are. When people who don't know you know more about you than your family does, I think that means you are famous."

"People don't know anything about me."

"For the last six years I've heard from you maybe two, three times a year. Out of respect for you I've never pushed you even when it was clear to me that things weren't as you said they were. I thought, maybe he has his reasons. Maybe you don't think it's important, but I didn't bring you up to send me a birth-day card and ignore me the rest of the year. It's disrespectful."

Alex looked at his father resentfully.

"I will make more of an effort dad. It's been a really difficult time. I'm sure you all think I have been gallivanting around all these years. But it hasn't been like that. At all. The opposite really."

"And why don't you ever call?"

"I didn't have a phone number until recently. I didn't want to bring you into my problems. I've just spent so much of my time putting out fires."

"You see, this is my point, Alex. It's like you are completely shut off from us. Like you don't want us to come in."

"It's not like that, dad."

"Well, what is it like then?"

"It's just too much to unpack right now dad. I've missed you. Missed mum."

"She'll be here soon enough," Oliviero said, his disappointment again evident.

"Well let's not waste any more time. Why don't you take me through your garden a bit and show me what you've been up to."

Over dinner, Alex wasn't surprised that he had less in common with his siblings than he did with their partners. Domenic and Sofia still enjoyed lobbing embarrassing stories about Alex's teenage years back and forth even if their partners were more interested in the meteoric months Alex was having.

His mum, Eleni, seemed pleased, no doubt happy to finally have her brood all under the one roof, but she rarely said anything to Alex. He noted however, that she was watching him constantly from the corner of her eye.

"Should we have dessert in the living room?" Sofia asked.

"No," Alex said, standing up and beginning to clear the plates "let's just have it here."

"Alex, leave them," Eleni said.

"No, it's no trouble," he replied, continuing the clearing.

"Let him do it," Domenic said, "it's not like he has to go to work tomorrow like the rest of us."

Alex let the comment slide even if others didn't.

"You know what?" Sofia asked, rhetorically. "We haven't had a family photo in years. Let's have some now before dessert. That way I can take them to the chemist downstairs from my office tomorrow and get reprints for everyone."

She smiled at Alex who smiled back at her.

Once they'd posed for a series of photos in all kinds of arrangements, Alex left the room, returning with the gifts he'd picked out for them in a Tokyo department store.

He was relieved he had bought something for everyone and watched as they excitedly unwrapped their gifts. But their excitement seemed to turn to shock.

"What's wrong?" Alex asked. "Have I done something wrong?"

"Alex, these are beautiful, but they're too extravagant," Domenic explained. "We can't accept these from you."

"Why not?"

"Because, well, they're a bit over the top aren't they? Can you really afford all this?"

Alex looked over the watches, scarves and cufflinks on the table and in his family's hands.

"Well Dom, consider it a wedding gift if it makes you feel more comfortable. Just pretend it only arrived all these years later."

"Alex, you've always had a problem understanding the value of money. Do you realise there's a small fortune in this room right now? That you're going to piss everything away really quickly if you don't grow up?"

"Fuck you Dom," Alex said, his parents calling for calm as the room erupted.

"Seriously fuck you. Nothing I ever do or say is good enough for you. If you don't want the cufflinks you can just shove them up your arse for all I care."

"Alex!" Eleni heaved. "Come on. Dom didn't mean it that way. He's just worried. We all worry about you."

"There's no need to worry about me. Anyway, I think I might just call a cab. It's been a long day. I'm going to head back to the hotel."

"Oh, please, don't go," Oliviero said, glaring at Domenic. "Not over something so petty."

"No really, I'm beat. And it's been lovely but I need to make a move. I have rehearsals tomorrow," he lied.

"We can give you a lift if you want," Patrick said, tilting his head. "It's not very far out of our way."

When Sofia looked at Alex pleadingly, he reluctantly accepted the offer.

Domenic relayed his goodbyes from the back porch, yelling something about seeing each other later in the week.

***

Alex's final days in Melbourne were packed with the second wave of his promotional duties. There was an instore appearance in the city centre which brought out a throng of teenagers, a couple of television interviews filmed at his hotel and studio performances for a popular Saturday night variety show and a weekly music show which aired on Sundays.

His family accompanied him to his television appearances, and though Alex had to return to the States, they later proudly called to tell him that *Burst* had finally entered the top ten in Australia and that it had achieved double platinum status shortly after.

After a seemingly endless run of singles, which culminated with another worldwide hit in February 1984, album sales ticked over six million copies worldwide, essentially forcing the hand of his label who were still undecided about the follow up.

| 7 |

PALM SPRINGS

When they first met, they were both at the mercy of unforgiving masters. Alex was a proverbial jack of all trades trying to land a break, Athena a young model already struggling to repeat her earlier successes.

She'd been booking work solidly since she was a teenager, but more and more was finding herself out of favour with the prevailing tastes of the times.

They became fast friends during his early years in New York. Without planning it, they ran into each other almost weekly at the downtown clubs and at makeshift parties on the Lower East Side.

At the time, he was gigging consistently, either with his own material or as a backing vocalist or dancer for all kinds of acts.

During those early years in New York their paths only converged by night, but one time, Alex finally saw Athena by daylight.

One sunny May day in 1982, he lay on the grass at Prospect Park after working a lunchtime shift at a restaurant, giving in to an urge for some sun. He'd pulled out the copy of *Nocturnes For The King Of Naples* that someone had given him and as he slowly read, found himself getting caught up in the novel's racy content and the pencil annotations he found on some of its pages.

But when he saw Athena walking nearby, he stood up and knocked over his Radio Shack transistor radio in doing so.

"Hey!" he yelled, not quite remembering her name. Andrea? Anthea? Athena. "Athena!"

She walked over smiling and gesticulating in surprise, waving her hands around and rolling her head back a little as if to say "what on earth are you doing here?" She gave him a peck on the cheek and asked if he was enjoying the sun.

"What are you doing in Brooklyn?" he asked, looking over his ancient, badly scuffed Ray Bans that he'd taken to with a felt pen to mask the scratches and paint flecks.

"A friend of mine lives near the park and I was having lunch with her."

"Oh great," he enthused, looking her over.

"No really, it was terrible. It was supposed to be a dry run for when she cooks for her boyfriend, but she hasn't got a chance. It was a nice gesture, but we decided it best she make a reservation somewhere instead. Anyway, what are you doing in Brooklyn?"

"Oh, I live here."

"Doesn't anyone live downtown anymore?" she asked rhetorically, looking him over.

"Is that where you live?" he asked, folding his arms over his bare chest.

"I live in the Village. Well, technically, I've been staying in the Village. One of the girls I work with is in London. I'm paying her share while she's away but it's not a real sublet. I have to find somewhere else soon. But you know what? I don't mind Brooklyn. I guess it's a lot cheaper out here."

He was curious to know about what she usually did with her days. She talked about modelling, as if to remind them both she had a profession, but explained she now worked part time in a commercial art gallery, where, she was "paid to simply be; to remind collectors and customers that it was a young and hip art space".

"I miss the financial freedom of modelling. I've been working since I was sixteen and they sent me here. But you know, the gallery scene isn't that different, it's full of people that are full of themselves."

"Well, there's no point in doing something if you're not passionate about it, right?" he said.

"Yeah, but it seems stupid that they all think it's so important. Like, when I was younger, the papers in Wollongong and Sydney were printing stories about how I was a 'success story' and an inspiration to young girls. Really? How so? By dropping out of school to have my picture taken? It's all a bit ridiculous. I just want to get to the point where I have enough money behind me that I can have a bit more consistency in life. Not always having to be at the whim of someone else's decisions."

"You know, you talk a lot," he said, smiling.

She blushed. "Oh, I know I do. *I do,* don't I? I can't help it... my friends tell me I could talk all day. Hey, I have to get the subway back to town. I've got a meeting with my agent."

"I'll walk you to the station."

"Yeah, sure, I mean, only if you're done here. It would be stupid for you to walk all that way, and then come back," she explained awkwardly, looking into his caramel eyes.

"No, I'm done here," he said, gathering his belongings.

He put his top back on and they continued talking while walking to the subway. They both had vague plans to pop in to *Club 57* or *Holiday* on Friday. As they said their goodbyes he leant in and kissed her on the lips, supplanting her cherry lip balm with his mix of gum and cigarettes. He smiled and waved, content he'd made her blush, and without bothering to wait as she passed through the turnstiles, simply turned around and walked off, Athena turning only to see the back of his head.

They did see each other that weekend, briefly at *Holiday*, where they kissed and flirted a little, but she had another party to go to, and he was staying put on account of his crew being all together for the first time in weeks.

After that, he didn't see her again for the longest time, and the machinations of his career kicked into gear shortly thereafter; landing him a semi–permanent gig at *57*, a runner up position in a NYC radio talent search, and eventually his record deals. Their paths didn't cross again until his debut album was just about to enter the charts.

Since moving on from Ben, he'd remained a free agent, his only regular beau, Allen, a Swiss engineer, who insisted on gifting Alex kitschy nationalistic t–shirts from his endless business trips abroad which Alex incorporated into his stage wardrobe.

When Alex and Athena finally ran into each other again, Alex was doing his final gig at *57*, which was heaving that night with an air of expectation. Alex was thankful that Jasper, Ian and Michael were present, all of them aware it could mark Alex's final official engagement in New York's underground scene.

"I haven't seen you in, forever. I thought you must have overdosed or something," Alex deadpanned when Athena approached him.

She smiled and pushed at him playfully.

"Nothing that dramatic. I've been in Montreal for the last year or so. Last dash of my modelling career before I have to retire from old age or something," she quipped.

"What are you doing back in New York?"

"I didn't know where else to go. And I figured I had to check your show out in person to see if you're the real deal."

Alex smiled. "So you're officially back in the city?"

"Just to get my things and say my goodbyes. I'm moving to LA for a bit. My agent got me a part in a soap. I'm officially an actress."

"An actress? God, the world is fucking fantastic. We need a drink to celebrate," he said, casually brushing Allen aside, who along with a friend was trying to join the conversation.

Alex waved the bartender over and ordered two shots which he and Athena then slammed down.

"You know my agent could probably set you up in LA. Get you some auditions. He's really good."

Alex laughed and kissed her on the cheek.

"I have to go downstairs. It's time. But give me your phone number. I want to see you before you leave New York. Before you turn into a coke fiend in Hollywood."

She smiled and pulled out a business card onto which she scrawled down a number. "I've got the couch for a few more days. Call me tomorrow."

He smiled and kissed her on the cheek before Michael arrived to lead him downstairs.

After the show was done, Alex ending it with a long speech in which he thanked everyone for their support, he returned to the VIP bar to look for Allen. He apologised for being so curt earlier and managed to convince Allen to follow him into a backroom, where, in the dark, he unbuckled Allen's belt and told him to turn around.

"Bend over a bit," Alex grunted, spitting into his palm.

***

When Alex arrived at the restaurant, he was dressed in his stage leggings from the night before and a crumbled up t–shirt he figured would regain its shape with his body heat. He felt un-derdressed but she'd chosen a place in the Village, so he figured he'd get away with the sloppy look. She was already there, look-ing amazing when he swaggered in with a coy smile, and his flaking Ray Bans.

"Congratulations on last night. You seemed to be having a ball. Everyone was," Athena said as he sat down after kissing her on the cheek.

"It's all a bit of a blur, but I think it went well," he said, pour-ing himself a glass of water.

"I'm booked for the red eye tomorrow. I have a million things to do. Mostly pack up my stuff really," she said.

"Are you excited about it?"

"Yeah. I guess since Montreal, I feel like New York doesn't feel like home anymore. I have no idea what LA is going to be like though."

"Be nice to be back by the coast again though." He thought for a moment. "*The Pacific.* It's in our systems you know."

"Yeah but you're from Melbourne. What would you know?"

"It's a state of mind. My family used to drive out to the coast every now and then. I miss that. I love New York but the only thing that bothers me is that the beaches aren't impressive." He poured himself another glass of water and downed it.

"Well now that you've got that big album contract you can come out and see me. We can go to the beach. You can surf. Hell, maybe even I will."

"Yeah you don't seem like the type who would be happy just watching her man do something."

"I didn't realise I was your woman Alex," she quipped.

"Oh I didn't mean it in that way," he said.

"What is it with you anyway? Everyone I ask has a different take on you," she stated, sipping on her water.

If she was frustrated by the idea, she wasn't letting on. He knew what she was referring to, of course.

"I don't have any hang ups I guess," he said. "I've been seeing a few people for a long time, and I'm a believer in just being upfront about those kinds of things. Everyone I'm with or have been with knows what I'm about."

"So, are you gay? Or just bi? Or, and sorry if I'm being so direct about this, I don't mean it in an insulting way. Are you going through an experimental phase?"

"I just don't see the point in putting myself in a box. I just date who I want to. I'm usually pretty good at reading the situation. I don't go looking for trouble despite what you might have heard about me."

She looked at her menu.

"I don't know if I could put myself in that kind of situation," she said. "I guess I'm more conventional than I like to think. I think monogamy is underrated and I think, it's all fine and well to talk in generalisations, but people need to be on the same page, otherwise it's a recipe for disaster."

"I think love is everywhere," Alex said. "It's not one specific thing. I don't get why people think it has to be one thing or another. Monogamy is fine, but I haven't been in that world for a long time," he said, his voice trailing off.

She didn't seem to want to volunteer anything, so he took it upon himself to do so.

"I think monogamy is a really noble thing. Like the highest possible form of respect that you can pay somebody. When I see you, I always get the impression you're somewhere else though. You're a ticket holder. You're always off somewhere… to another party, to Montreal or LA. I don't know how that sits with monogamy. How would you make that work?"

"Well if you want it to work, you make it work," she said, snapping her menu shut.

"Wouldn't you be better off concentrating on what things are like with someone before worrying about monogamy?"

"Said like someone always looking to get laid," she said, something like a laugh following the statement.

"Trust me, I wouldn't bother with all this polite chitchat if I was just looking to get laid."

"What would you do then?" she asked, her eyebrow raised.

"To have sex with you?"

"Yep."

"I'd tell you that in the time it took for you to choose your entrée I could have already made you come. But if you'd prefer to sit here and have a pleasant lunch rather than go straight back to yours, I'm okay with that."

"We can't do both?" she asked, smiling.

"I can," he said, "I'm not the one with a flight tomorrow."

***

Despite their bicoastal status, Athena and Alex managed to spend a good deal of time together once Alex returned from his whirlwind press junket. She bunked down with him at his NYC rental and he at hers in LA whenever her agenda allowed it.

He never let her know it, but she'd become his first official girlfriend.

In her company, he was a slightly more settled version of himself, content to follow one side of his heart to its logical conclusion. In him she saw the chance to live on the wilder side of things; he was challenging and unconventional, but he communicated with her in a way that no other man had before.

Though he was concentrating on writing for the next album, it seemed much of the beginning of 1984 was overshadowed by the ongoing success of *Burst*. Despite being snubbed in the critical categories, Alex received a slew of nominations during the awards season, mostly in recognition of his success on the singles charts. With Athena by his side, he attended a number of ceremonies but walked away empty handed from them all.

The two of them wrangled invites to a few after parties where Alex felt more comfortable rubbing shoulders than he did at the televised events he'd been called upon to present at.

At the parties Athena saw a new side to him.

"Just try and relax," she cooed as he stood stuck in his tracks at one Hollywood restaurant.

"I think I just need a drink," he admitted.

"Someone will bring them over," she promised.

"What am I supposed to say to people?"

"Just say hello. Start from there. But you need to relax. You're all stiff."

"I don't get why you're so relaxed," he said, relieved when a waiter came by with a tray of glasses, which he helped himself to.

"I've been to a million of these kinds of things. They're all the same," she said, thanking him as he handed her a flute glass.

"When's Michael getting here?"

"Relax babe, shall we go outside for a cigarette?"

Outside he struck up a conversation with a fellow record label mate who he knew from New York. Like his, her debut album had recently blown up and she explained the label had just offered her a huge advance for the follow up.

"They'll do the same for you, I know it," she said.

***

After weeks of back and forth with Michael's office, Alex and Michael were convened to a meeting at the label's LA offices, where Alex largely deferred to Michael as usual.

Talk turned to taking a change in musical direction to widen Alex's audience.

Although he was now considered something of a priority act, it was no secret that the label expected to be heavily involved in the second album's development.

"Michael, I know you had a list of producers that the two of you came up with," Sam, one of the label Vice Presidents said. "But I don't think the budget is going to stretch that far. We've been talking with Daniel Millard. He's really hot right now and he's available."

"Millard's thing is rock. That's not Alekzandr's thing."

"We're keen for Alekzandr to broaden his sound a bit. We're just not prepared to have him and Ian do it alone. There's too much riding on it."

Alex wanted to say something, but Michael put his hand on Alex's forearm.

"Yes, but significantly less than the numbers you mentioned last week," Michael said.

"I couldn't get it to stick Michael. We're taking Alekzandr's project very seriously, but you know as well as I do that the bottom is already falling out of disco. Meet with Millard. He's here in LA. He's got some great ideas. We can talk again once you've spoken with Daniel."

In the elevator, Alex looked at Michael angrily.

"What the hell am I supposed to say to Ian? I thought it was a sure thing that we'd get to do it ourselves this time."

"I know kid," Michael said, looking at Alex earnestly. "I really thought it was going to go our way. I hate to agree with Sam, but he made a good point. Maybe you should both work with other people for a bit."

"It feels shitty. They didn't know what they were doing the first time around. It was largely thanks to me and Ian that things went the way they did."

"I know," Michael said, putting his hand on Alex's shoulder. "Let's just meet with the guy and see what he has to say. And if you want, I'll talk to Ian for you."

"No. I need to do that myself."

"He's a sharp kid. He'll get it. I might be able to line something else up for him anyway," Michael said, ushering Alex out of the lift.

The following day they met with Millard and Millard's agent. Millard played a few of his demos for everyone and listened intently to those that Alex and Ian had prepared.

"There's a lot of potential in these," Millard said. "I think I see where you're going with them."

"I like what you've done on Howard's record," Alex said.

"Oh, you've heard it already?"

"Yesterday," Alex replied. "Here."

"Well I wouldn't try and do the same thing with you. I think we could come up with something different together."

"Different is good," Alex agreed.

"There's just one thing, and I didn't say anything to Sam and the team. But my daughter's started school in London. I can't do the project here like I did Howard's."

Alex looked at Michael. He didn't want Michael to say anything. To affirm anything. To agree to anything.

"That's going to eat into the budget," Michael stated.

"But I've got my band there, who'll be great for this album."

"Still going to suck up a fair bit of money from our side," Michael said, directing the comment to Millard's agent. "Why don't you two go and get some air and leave us suits here to chat."

"Great," Millard said, "I'm dying for a cigarette anyway."

"I'm going to stay," Alex said. "You go ahead."

***

While Alex was in New York to ostensibly pack for London, he took Ian out for a ritzy dinner where he broke the news that they wouldn't be producing the album together.

"I had a feeling you were going to leave me stranded on this one," Ian said.

"Michael promised me he was going to find you something. And then he told me he was working on something for all of us."

"And you trust him?"

"Yeah, implicitly."

"God Alex, you're so naïve sometimes."

"Why?"

"He'll say anything. He never delivers like you say he does you know. He just wants to get into your pants," Ian said, angrily.

"What are you on about?" Alex said, his cheeks stinging.

"But I suspect you get off on that."

"Dude, what's gotten into you?" Alex asked.

"Nothing Alex, I'm just pissed that you're already selling yourself out. Selling me out."

"It's not true Ian."

"I don't know if I even want our songs on your album to be honest."

"Stop being an idiot," Alex warned him.

"Maybe I need to get my own manager. Someone that's gonna kiss my arse and be prepared to cast off everyone else around me."

"Come on, it's not like that."

"It is Alex," Ian said, standing up and putting on his jacket. "Do what you want with those songs. Michael's already fucked me over with everything he had me sign anyway."

Alex watched as Ian stormed out of the restaurant.

He looked at his watch and asked a waiter if he could use the phone.

"Any seats left on the red eye?" Alex asked when someone finally responded.

***

Arriving in LA, Alex spent a few days with Athena who had wrapped up work on her soap and was about to begin work on her first film.

She took him out to Palm Springs, where during a spa treatment she made Alex a completely out of the box proposition. He laughed on hearing it, but when he realized she was completely serious, the rest of their time in Palm Springs turned awkward.

On the last day, she drove him directly to LAX, the car shrouded in silence. When they arrived, he finally turned to her.

"Give me some time to think about it," he said.

"Don't keep me hanging Alex."

"I won't," he said, gathering the belongings at his feet and fumbling somewhat to open the door.

| 8 |

LONDON II

Landing in London, he felt emotional. The last visits he'd made there had been mad whirls of hotel rooms, TV and radio stations and the once off performance at Brixton Academy to promote the first album.

On his way to his lodgings, it occurred to him that he was being supplanted somewhere familiar where he no longer belonged. It irritated him. During all that time in New York, he'd seen London as his blueprint. It had been cruel to him at times but he was proud of having momentarily carved out a niche for himself there.

Still, it was tough being asked to step back into his past to prepare for his future. If all went well, he'd have a new album to show for it, but he had to decide about just how much he wanted to get back in contact with his old friends. Seeing his old mates at Brixton gig had been awkward. More than a few of them had used the night to accuse him of being a sell out.

Now that his royalties were finally starting to come in, Michael also warned him to be wary of old friends. Something about a gravy train.

After a night in his new dwellings, Alex nonetheless decided to test the waters. He figured he'd start with Terri, his old friend who'd always generously offered up her couch when he needed it. He dialled her number from memory and was slightly aghast when she picked up after just a ring.

"Terri is that you?"

"Alex? Where are you?"

"I'm in Shoreditch. I've got a house here for a while."

"When did you arrive?" she asked.

"Yesterday. Can I see you?"

"Are you kidding? Of course. When my love?"

"Anytime. If you want to do dinner tonight, I'm free."

"You know I had plans to… no, fuck that, yes. *Yes*! Do you want to come to me and we'll go to the Prince?"

It hadn't been quite what Alex had in mind, but the old local they'd routinely hit on weekends for a cheap feast seemed as good a place as any to reunite in.

Annoyed by how the record label had stocked his larder, Alex spent the morning at the local Tesco and the rest of the day writing corrections into his lyric book before sauntering out into the boroughs. He caught the tube part of the way and found himself walking through the familiar streets of Terri's area. It was exactly as he remembered it. He'd missed the misty, fresh spring nights in Brockley, his unofficial home away from home (away from home).

He rasped on the door of the brick single, and just like on the phone, was startled by how quickly Terri answered.

"Were you waiting at the door for me?" he sneered. "Fuck you look good, you cow," he said, kissing her on both cheeks.

"You look good enough to eat my little cup cake," she smiled. "Oh my gosh, look at you. Your hair's black! God it's cold tonight, I'm going to freeze my tits off, come in, come in!"

They sized each other up, Alex noting how fantastic she looked. She was in shape and blonder than ever. The house also looked like it had been improved. He noticed 'his' old sofa was gone, replaced by a velour one in a strange olive tone. Elsewhere he spied other 1950s styled furniture.

"New York suits you. You've lost all your puppy fat," she gushed. "God Alex, you even smell good for a change," she laughed, following him into the kitchen. "Oh my God. I need to know everything," she said, bringing the gin bottle down from the freezer.

"No," he said. "You first."

She talked about teaching and life in general, but he found himself more interested in how she'd been dating a banker for over a year now and that they'd even set a wedding date for the summer.

"I had to make my peace with our old life," she said sadly, clinking her tumbler with his. "I barely see anyone from the past. I do hear from some of them from time to time. Usually when they want something. Still complete disasters if you ask me."

She sipped from her glass. "You know, you're not saying much my love. Are you okay?"

"Yeah, I'm just taking it in," he said, apologetically. "It's a lot, you know. It's mostly good. But being back here in London… it's thrown me."

"You'll work it out. Give yourself a chance to readjust. You've always been so impatient."

"I feel bad though," he said. "I don't know if I want to see anyone from the past. Maybe Marin or Shelly? But Shelly got all weird on me in Brixton."

"Well Marin's moved back to Stockholm," she said, tentatively.

"And Shelly?" Alex asked.

She didn't answer.

"Do you not hear from her anymore?" Alex asked.

"Alex, Shelly's gone."

"Where?"

"She's *gone*."

"What do you mean gone? Gone where?"

"Oh God," Terri said. "I thought you already knew."

"Knew what? Did she go back to Scotland?"

"No sweetheart," she said, sadly. "She passed away. A few months ago."

Alex's head began shaking erratically. "Terri, what are you saying?" he finally asked.

Terri clucked her tongue and apologised. "The coroner was inconclusive. They said she might have had heart failure but they couldn't rule out an overdose. Her boyfriend found her days later."

Alex sat himself down at the laminate table. He looked at all the specks in the surface. He didn't want to continue the conversation. Wanted to go. Anywhere.

They never made it to the pub that night and, as on so many other occasions in his life, Alex slept on Terri's couch even if he barely got a wink of sleep.

In the morning he accompanied her to the station and then decided to walk all the way back home. Didn't care how long it would take.

At the house he called Athena to check in. She talked at length about how things were going on the set and how she'd found a house that she was about to make an offer on. How she wanted him to see it. She was so full of commitments and plans that he could barely get a word in edgewise.

"Listen Alex, I have to go, I've got to get ready for a fitting."

"Okay," he said, "but I just want to say that if the offer still stands, then the answer is yes."

***

For the first week in the studio, many of the discussions with Millard, the producer, flew over Alex's head. He was distracted by his thoughts about Shelly, and Millard's technical conversations only made him anxious, reminding him that he was on his own and that he had much to learn.

Heeding Michael's warning, Alex kept a low profile, deciding to wait for Michael's arrival rather than seek out any old friends in the interim. After an awkward first week in the studio and a quiet weekend mostly spent with Terri and her fiancé, Alex returned to the studio.

Millard proved a taskmaster who asked Alex to rewrite or re-arrange his song parts over and over. Though Alex found it frustrating to have to consider his songs from a producer's point of view, deep down, he knew he needed to begin regarding his producer as more than just a technical turnkey.

So after making countless changes to his songs, he decided it would be more helpful to treat the album as an apprenticeship. Almost overnight, he began paying close attention to what Millard did, his sudden interest throwing the producer for a loop. But soon enough Millard was coaching him, making instructive comments about the soundboard, managing musicians and the benefits of being meticulous in the studio.

As Alex's understanding of the technical side grew, so too did the burdens of his opinions. As a result, tensions rose, the two often locked in heated debate for hours at a time about the direction some songs were taking. By the time they'd completed the first half of the album, their collaborative honeymoon was well and truly over.

They still had five more songs to work on. Alex had been looking forward to working on two of them in particular; *Just Us,* a song sourced from an up and coming singer/songwriter, and *Dangerous,* which he'd had written with Ian. He had high hopes for them both but Millard insisted they tease out the songs' glam rock aspects which Alex loathed. After a week of intense disagreement and stand offs, work effectively came to a halt, Millard so enraged by Alex's stubbornness, that he threatened to walk away from the project.

Despite the intervention of the British A&R leg, the impasse was proving insurmountable, Millard refusing to return to the studios, and Alex refusing to budge. It was only with Michael's arrival in London two weeks later that negotiations resumed.

"You're both acting like schoolboys on a playground," Michael said, furious that Alex was beaming at the label's boardroom table. "Can I suggest you both go back to work tomorrow and begin polishing the songs from the first batch. Once they're in order, the direction of the new ones will become clearer to you both."

In the end it was the threat of legal action that dragged Millard back into the studio, but after only three days, it became clear that the two couldn't even agree to the tiniest of details, and Millard finally upped and left the studio in a flurry of expletives, taking his personal belongings with him.

"Are you satisfied?" Michael said, arriving at the studio later that day. "There's going to be a shit storm."

"I don't care," Alex said, defiantly lighting a cigarette. "He was getting too big for his boots."

"*He* was? You know, time is money and your money has been paying for an empty studio these last few weeks. And for a producer who won't produce for you. Call him back in. Swallow your pride."

"Not gonna do that."

"God, Alex, there are times when I could just deck you."

"You know Michael, you and he both would do well to remember that you both work for me. Not the other way around."

"It's not that cut and dry Alex. You'd best remember that."

"I need some air," Alex said, packing his own things and abandoning Michael in the control room.

Back at his rental, Alex made the call he'd been making daily since he'd started work in the studio.

"And he's not coming back this time?" Ian asked, over the crackly line.

"Nope. It's done," Alex said. "But I don't know how long we've got. Michael's making things more complicated."

"Fuck him. Literally," Ian said. "It's what he wants. And it'll buy us more time if you've got Michael onside."

"Just get your arse over here as quickly as you can," Alex said.

The moment Ian landed at Heathrow and hightailed it to the studio, the two of them worked day and night. Michael was locked in negotiations with Millard's representation, and was so angry with Alex that he barely took his calls.

Desperate to get as much recording done as they could, Alex reached out to some old musician friends, who demanded they be paid in cash daily for the ten and twelve hour long recording sessions Alex and Ian put them through. In the nine days that they worked non-stop, the boys managed to construct solid portions of the five songs left. But entering the control room on the tenth day, the boys were frozen in their tracks.

"Care to explain all this?" Michael asked from behind the control deck, motioning to all the notes the boys had stuck over the panel, Millard watching them from the sofa.

"While I've been negotiating in good faith, you've gone and taken things into your own hands. What were you thinking? And what the hell are you doing here, Ian?"

"Well it's not like I could just sit around waiting for him to stop throwing a tantrum," Alex said, leering at Millard.

"Listen kid, we have a contract," Millard said. "You can't just go around doing what you want when it suits you."

"Funny, I could say the same thing to you," Alex replied.

"Michael all the stuff they've done, you've heard it this morning. It's second rate. If the label goes for it, I don't want my name associated with any of it. I've put up with enough of his nonsense."

"I am here in the room, you know?" Alex said, angrily.

"Alex put a lid on it," Michael said, sighing and kneading his temples.

"This changes everything," Millard said, pointing to the control deck.

Michael cupped his head in his hands.

"I guess it's back to the lawyer's offices," Michael said, exhausted.

***

Despite the reprimands, Alex and Ian wasted no time in resuming work, more motivated than ever to finish what they'd started. That week, Alex's presence in the studio was frequently interrupted, summoned repeatedly to the record label offices to be dressed down and to mediation meetings with Millard's representatives. When he refused to backdown, knowing Millard had no intention of respecting his ideas, Alex was also subjected to Michael and the A&R team's impromptu visits to the studio, which inevitably resulted in threats made about having his album advance cut or withdrawn.

When the label came through with their threat to withdraw funding, Alex made arrangements with the recording studio to pay for the remaining studio time he and Ian needed out of his own pocket.

Satisfied with what they'd achieved, the boys flew out of London feeling like fugitives. Alex knew he'd be made to face the music once he was back in the States, but he was happy to be on his way, also looking forward to seeing Athena again. During the flight he chuckled as he confessed to Ian that he'd never been so celibate before in his entire life. He felt he'd owed Athena at least that.

***

"I know how ridiculous it is," she'd said, back in Palm Springs. "We'll probably never get to spend any time together. But we know what we mean to each other," she'd said, sitting on the living room floor. "And we can both keep a secret. No one has to know. But you and I will. All the shit can hit the fan, but at the end of the day you'll be my husband, and I'll be your wife."

The idea had made Alex laugh at first. It seemed childish to him. But in time, he understood the logic and the comfort behind it.

She'd finished work on the film and had made him howl with laughter when she'd called him once he was well and truly back from London.

"I'm about to leave for Minneapolis," she said.

"Why? What's there?"

"A recording studio. I'm a singer now."

He practically spat out his tea. "Are you serious? God, that's fucking brilliant. Who are you going to be working with?"

"I've never really heard of them. But one of the girls on the soap told me about them. They specialise in pop songs for the

Japanese market. Apparently, they love me on the soap over there and they want to capitalise on that."

"God, I think I need your agent," Alex said.

"They asked me to ask if you had a couple of songs that you'd be prepared to give us. Me. Them. I don't know."

"I'll have to run it by Michael. He still manages mine and Ian's affairs, but I don't know for how much longer."

"Oh Michael. How is he? Has he calmed down yet?"

"No, he's still furious with me. Anyway, how long are you going to be in Minneapolis for?"

"Oh, they said I just had to come in for a couple of meetings and then they'd organise a schedule for me to record the songs. They'll call me when they're ready for me."

"Jesus," Alex said. "And you're okay with all that? Putting something out for the sake of it?"

"Alex, I'm not a singer. Besides, it's just for Japan and they said they could do all kinds of things in the studio and that I don't have to worry. You should see the money they're prepared to pump into it all. It's crazy."

"When will you be in New York?"

"At the end of the week. My manager is making all the arrangements for us. Just stay out of trouble this week. I'll be there soon, I promise."

***

It was the first piece of property he'd ever owned. Members of the co-op had voiced their opposition to his buying in, concerned that having a popstar in their midst would impinge on their daily lives. But Alex's offer to buy out the entire top floor was approved, nonetheless.

Renovation work had been carried out while he was in London, Alex almost entirely wiping out his bank account to pay for it.

He spent his first week back putting things in order, anxious that he wasn't going to have enough money to actually furnish the place, especially after the London debacle.

Ian was staying with him, waiting out the refurbishing work on his own first purchase; a villa in Miami.

When the doorbell buzzed, Alex figured it was him, and that, like always, he'd slipped past the doorman with an apology for forgetting his keys again. Alex opened the door, prepared to deliver his usual sermon about Ian's forgetfulness, but was stopped in his tracks.

"Did you think hiding out here was going to make all your problems disappear?"

"Michael."

"Are you going to let me in?"

Alex's heart sank. "Of course," he said, opening the door wide and ushering Michael in.

"It's looking good," Michael said, looking around. "Bit dusty though."

"I'm working on it," Alex said, closing the door behind him.

"So, ask me where I've been all day."

Alex looked him over. "Okay. Where?"

"At your record label. You're bloody lucky they don't have your new number yet."

"I can explain."

"Oh, I'm not interested in your explanations," Michael said, opening the fridge and helping himself to a beer. "I'm not here for your apologies for hanging me out to dry while I cleaned up your mess for you. I'm not even here to understand why you left London without so much as a word to me. For a minute I thought you were back with your old buddies there. That on top of everything else, I also needed to worry that you were passed out in some drug den."

"That's a bit dramatic," Alex said, getting himself a beer.

"Oh no. That's not the dramatic part of it. You'll want to sit down for this."

Alex looked at Michael nervously.

"In your absence, your record label has decided that you've breached the terms of the contract that you have with them. The little stunt that you and Ian pulled in London has just cost you tens of thousands of dollars."

"What?"

"Yep," Michael said, ruefully. "Millard is getting paid out in full. Yours and Ian's recordings need to be reworked because the label agrees with Millard that they're not up to par. And you're not going to meet the deadline to get it all done in time for the scheduled release date."

"What does that mean?"

"It means that they're going to garnish your royalties until they recover all the extra costs. And that in the end, the stuff you and Ian did is going to be handed over to someone else to fix."

"That's bullshit."

"No, I warned you Alex. I told you that time is money. Your money."

"I want a meeting with them."

"It would only create more problems. You're on thin ice with them. Again. They said it's worse this time around. Said you practically pulled the same shit with them with *Burst*."

"I'm sorry," Alex said, fingering his beer can.

"They won't care about that."

"No. I'm sorry. For you. I didn't mean to put you in that position Michael, I swear."

"I've spent the last two weeks with everyone breathing down my neck," Michael said, clearly hurt. "For you. And you just disappeared on me. After everything I've done for you."

"Are you resigning?" Alex asked, defeated.

"I should. You won't be able to pay me for a while. If you're lucky," Michael said, looking around the apartment.

Alex crossed his arms deep into his chest. "What if Ian and I fix things? What if we have a meeting and do what they want to the songs. That way we don't have to pay someone else to do it."

"I don't know if they'll go for that. The studio time is still going to cost you. They won't front you any money for you to do it."

"You saw how quickly we got things done. We can do it. I'll find the money."

Michael looked at Alex. "Listen kid. I've been thinking. If we get through this, we have to change things up. I've been thinking about it for ages. But this album has to work. It has to sell. And you have to get them back on side, otherwise there's no point in taking the next step."

"What next step?"

"I'll tell you when the time is right. But right now, you have to listen to me. Do what I tell you. I'll set up the meeting, but no more theatrics. No more of this diva shit. And give this place a good clean up. I worked my arse off to convince them to let you buy in. Don't make me look a fool."

***

During a five day break from Minneapolis, Athena flew back into New York as promised.

Alex headed to the address as instructed and met her and the elderly couple from Athena's old apartment block. The couple, who were completely oblivious to the rising stars, agreed to act as witnesses, watching quietly as the two were declared husband and wife under a giant American flag inside city hall.

Despite his nerves, it felt like the right thing to do.

The ceremony was quick and painless, its ending giving the two of them a rush. Right after their ceremony, they headed out to the airport and boarded a chartered flight to Puerto Rico for a three day honeymoon.

The only acknowledgement they made of their new marital status, aside from the two matching Polaroids they had snapped at the ceremony, was in the matching ear piercings they had done in San Juan. They had a chemist's assistant feed matching diamond stud earrings into their left ears and celebrated afterwards at their beachfront hotel, from which they never stepped out until it was time to take their flights; hers to Minneapolis and his to NYC. Those three days were spent lounging about, making love and eating. Moments that were constantly interspersed with giddy, complicit excitement that they had finally done it.

As soon as he arrived back at his new home in New York he placed two calls. The first was to Athena's Minneapolis number to check in and congratulate her on becoming his wife. The second was more like the barking of orders. "What are you doing?... aha... well, when you're finished doing that, come over to my apartment. I need to talk to you."

Michael arrived later that afternoon, as instructed.

"Funche! I haven't seen this brand since I was a kid."

"The woman in the shop said it was the best."

"But you can't get this brand in the States. Where have you been?"

"Puerto Rico. I needed a couple of days of R&R."

"But you're whiter than ever."

"I just mostly hung out in the hotel," Alex said. "Anyway, I was thinking of you while I was there. Of how much of an arsehole I've been to you. And I wanted to say sorry again. And that I've come up with the money."

"Ian?"

"No."

"Ah. Athena," Michael said, not bothering to disguise his disappointment.

"Look, it doesn't matter where I got the money. I just wanted you to know that I'm going to fix things. I can't imagine doing any of this without you Michael," Alex said, haltingly. "You've kept every one of your promises to me and I hate that I've let you down. You don't deserve that."

Michael studied Alex for a moment. "Are you alright kid?"

"Yeah. I've just been thinking. Sometimes I get carried away and don't think about things until it's too late," Alex said.

"Is there something you want to tell me?" Michael asked.

Alex faked a smile. "No Estes, everything's alright. I promise."

"Don't make me worry about you more than I already do."

"You don't need to worry about me," Alex said softly.

"I do though," Michael said, resting his hand on Alex's over the kitchen counter. "You and I are in this together. All the way."

Alex was sure he heard a quiver in Michael's voice. He knew the moment was now his to do whatever he pleased.

"Anyway, I just wanted to say thanks and sorry," Alex said, finally. "To clear the air with a bit of funche. Puerto Rican style."

Michael stepped away from the counter.

"Do you want me to cook some up for you?"

"Are you mad? I wouldn't touch that stuff with a bargepole," Alex said, smiling.

"You don't know what you're missing."

"Story of my life."

| 9 |

MAGIC

Alex spent the early Summer in the studio with Ian, acquiescing to the label's demands. Occasionally he was called into the label's offices by the creative directors to approve changes to the album's cover art and discuss ideas for the first music video, which Jasper had agreed to direct.

There was some concern about Alex's new dark haired look and lingering concern about how the album might be a little too *European* for American radio. Alex thought the label's commentary and paranoia was hilarious, but he played nice just as he'd promised Michael.

Athena's album was already a hit in Japan, her allure as a film and television actress encouraging radio elsewhere to pick up some of her songs. Though they'd never been intended for American audiences, her label had her out on the publicity trail across North America and Asia.

After getting the label to sign off on his own album and video, Alex found himself at a loss as to what to do with the rest of his summer. With Athena crisscrossing the Pacific, Alex, newly flush with another round of royalties, decided to reward himself with a holiday in the Greek isles. Unfortunately, Jasper had a film to work on and Ian was tied up in Miami with the joys of home ownership, so Alex was on his own.

He called into Michael's office and left a print out of the itinerary that the travel agent had prepared for him. He then called Athena, promising he'd be back by the end of August. She seemed delighted that he was taking a break for himself, mentioning that she would've joined him were she not required on set the minute her promotional tour was over.

Alex spent his first night in Athens, and the following morning, he walked around the quarter until he found a barber shop. He'd woken that morning deciding it was too hot to bother with shoulder length hair.

Settling down without a word, Alex pointed to the picture of George Hamilton stuck to the mirror. The barber nodded and made quick work of Alex's hair, shearing it down to the shortest it had been in six years. Alex looked at himself in the mirror with curiosity, smiled, paid and walked back out onto the street, lighter than ever.

He spent close to a week wandering the city with his camera and notebook, spending his days being ferried out to beaches, and his nights surveying the city on foot, occasionally stopping for a drink or a cocktail. His hotel was discreet and had a pool, and its relaxed staff never bothered him when it was too hot to head out and explore the city.

After Athens he set off on a two week trip around the islands, checking into all manner of hotels and seeking out the most isolated of beaches where he could be alone and undisturbed. He read of *Dorian Gray* and of *Maurice* and sketched and wrote.

Though there were times when he pined for some company, he was relieved to finally have some alone time for the first time in years. He thanked his lucky stars that Michael had forced him to get his driver's license all those months earlier, as he felt that the islands would have lost their sheen had he not been able to move around them independently.

He knew the islands were just a big distraction on his part; a way to stave off the anxiety over what lay next. Occasionally he allowed himself the luxury of realising how far he'd come since leaving Melbourne. He knew he should pinch himself for finally having found his purpose; as someone who made music and sold records.

But the arrival of the afternoon's headwinds signalled it was time to head back to the hotel. There, without the full force of the Mediterranean attempting to pull him away from his thoughts, he found himself thinking about the same thing, night in, night out. *Michael.* All the time. Had done so ever since he'd been sitting at the boarding gate in San Jose, feeling like he'd made a huge mistake. From that day forth, he'd spent many a night lying in bed, conjuring up Michael's image. That strong nose, those green eyes, the dark, wavy hair. He knew that if he lined up a thousand lookalikes, he'd have no trouble identifying *his* Michael.

He loved the idea that Michael was his protector. Loved how Michael's dominating nature was always tempered by a sweet side. Loved the sense of security that Michael gave him, Michael's words always sheathed in confidence.

Alex didn't think of Athena with any of the same intensity. She didn't seem to tap into that part of his psyche. In truth, he rarely thought of her during those long, hot days. Maybe sometimes when he caught a glimpse of himself in the mirror and saw the shining diamond stud in his ear. But she didn't captivate his imagination. Didn't command his thoughts the way Michael so easily did. Didn't propel him to jerk off while thinking about her. He had to be with her to experience her. To appreciate her. But with Michael it was *different*. Just the thought of him was enough to help Alex gush out a load before falling asleep, contented.

***

On his return to New York, he unwrapped the one package among all the mail that awaited him. It was a vinyl copy of his new LP, fresh from the first pressings.

He studied the cover art. Barely recognised himself under the spiky goth wig and the heavy kohl. But he was more interested in something else. He flipped the cover and saw them; his first ever proper production credits.

As he began fumbling over the record player, the phone rang. It was Athena. Filming in Nevada was going to be pushed out for a few more weeks.

"Have you seen the charts?" she asked.

"No. I just literally got back into the apartment. My new record arrived."

"Did they deliver your copy of Billboard?"

"I think so," he said, irritated by her tone.

"Open it. I'll wait."

"What am I looking for?"

But she didn't need to answer. He found it. Billboard spelled it out for him. She'd achieved something he hadn't yet; a top five hit. Even had a second single in the top ten.

"Gosh," he said, smiling. "Athena! You're a fucking over-achiever. Have you celebrated?"

"Yeah. Last night a bunch of us hit Reno."

"Well, the way things are going you're going to have to celebrate again next week. You're going to have another top five hit!"

"They're already talking about me recording another album. I don't know when I'm going to find the time to do it."

"You'll make the time. You need to strike while the iron's hot, right?"

"Yeah, that's what my manager says. Anyway, how was Greece? Did you miss me?"

"It was great," he said. "Lots."

"Listen, I have to go. I'm being told the catering's ready. I'll talk to you soon."

"Yeah," he replied, but she'd already hung up.

He cued up the stylus and cracked open a beer, listening to Side A, full of his tracks with Millard.

As he listened to the songs, they sounded different, especially now that they were pounding out of his speakers and his voice was floating around the apartment. As he listened, he looked at the inner sleeve, scanning for errors.

All told the Millard tracks were *okay*. He didn't love them but didn't hate them either.

He flipped the disc and lit himself a cigarette, crashing down onto the new sofa which had arrived in his absence.

There was only one Millard song on this side, the opener, and once it was done, he concentrated on his and Ian's handiwork. It didn't have the sheen Millard's work did but he liked it. Liked that the album was finally sounding like it had a bit of edge. A bit of grunt despite the electronic sounds.

Listening to the album in this way made him worry a little. Side A and Side B really felt like two different records. He hoped he would pull it off. For everyone's sakes.

After a few days of avoiding Michael's calls, for no reason other than wanting a bit more calm before the storm, Alex relented and visited his office. He felt self–conscious, as if Michael was looking through him, aware of how many times Alex had jerked off to the idea of him.

In actual fact, Michael was equally disturbed by seeing him. "You've cut your hair."

"You don't like it?" Alex asked, concerned.

"You've been avoiding me."

"I haven't. Well. Maybe. A little. I'm just feeling a bit overwhelmed by everything."

"Maybe it's just nerves," Michael said, smiling.

"I'm sure it is," Alex said.

"All the promo stuff is about to kick off. Are you ready for it? With that tan of yours that's going to give your A&R guy another coronary."

He knew that in a matter of days, Michael would begin pushing him into the promotional machine. That they'd be in each other's pockets again for the foreseeable future and that he'd need to keep a lid on things, even though he knew, just as his closest friends did, that he and Michael both wanted the same thing.

"I'm okay. I just need to get through the first day of it all and everything will be alright. I promise."

***

His September quickly got out of control. The single, *Magic,* had been sent to radio the week he'd gotten back from Europe. More ethereal and less club oriented than anything he'd recorded before, it seemed to intrigue the record buying public even if it hadn't really won over the critics.

After a solid fortnight of press, Alex went into rehearsal mode for the first annual MTV Video Music Awards. By the time Alex appeared on stage at Radio City Music Hall for the show, at which he'd been nominated for two awards, the single was already climbing the chart.

Miles, his key dancer from way back, had devised the choreography for the performance and was one of the two backing dancers who accompanied Alex as he sang against a backing track.

Alex's new, unplanned, darker look seemed to coincide with the direction his music was taking. But a mere glance around the hall made it clear that short spiky hair, a heavy eye and a touch of lipstick were now de rigueur. On camera he explained his new sound was "like a poppier version of the music that Cocteau Twins and Dead Can Dance were making."

Audiences in the US responded reasonably well to the single and it peaked at No.9 in November, a couple of rungs behind Athena's latest single (which he and Ian had penned). The album, *Magic,* was pushed into stores in November, quickly ascending into the top ten and remaining there for the Christmas season, keeping company with a slew of pop releases by Hall & Oates, Wham!, Madonna and Prince.

Although they had gotten off to a good start in North America, the music had faltered elsewhere, particularly in the UK and Australia, where the single and album languished in the lower reaches of the charts after receiving mixed reviews. The perception was that in having moved away from his Kerala club sound, Alekzandr had left his strengths behind.

Far from getting ready to enjoy the Christmas/New Year period, Alex was pushed back onto the international promotional trail. Before leaving, he filmed two hastily prepared music videos in New York; one, an inoffensive performance piece filmed in a Queens bar for *Just Us,* and the other a striking, monochromatic clip for *Dangerous* built around a sexy choreographic piece designed by Miles. *Dangerous* would become his first truly iconic video, later copied and tributed by dozens of artists throughout the 1980s and 1990s.

To sure up the international sales, the label organised a promotional tour beginning in December, the itinerary including Europe, the Asia Pacific and Latin America. The budget only allowed for Alex and Michael to travel, forcing Alex to work with studio dancers for all his television appearances.

The schedule was tighter than it had been for the *Burst* promotion. In the space of ten days, Alex and Michael steamed through London, Paris, Barcelona and West Berlin.

In West Berlin, their engagements coincided with Athena's, whose single was out–charting his across Europe. The music press was abuzz the following week when paparazzi shots of the two of them leaving one of West Berlin's hottest clubs together were published.

After pit stops in Zurich and Milan, Alex and Michael high-tailed it by train to Vienna, where somehow Alex had been invited to perform on the televised *Heiligenabend* concert on Christmas Eve.

On Christmas morning, Alex knocked on Michael's door.

"Merry Christmas," Alex said, handing Michael a small, wrapped package. Michael looked at it, the gold and red trim making him smile.

"What is it?"

"Well, you'll have to open it if you want to find out," Alex said, letting himself in. The room smelt a little stale with hints of cigarette smoke and musk.

"I didn't get you anything. I feel terrible," Michael said.

"Buy me a drink and we'll call it even," Alex said, peeking through the curtains at the snowcapped roofs below him.

Michael obliged, emptying out what was left of the minibar.

"What time do we fly out today anyway?"

"Not 'til nine tonight," Michael said, handing Alex a tumbler.

"Well, aren't you going to open it?" Alex asked.

"I kind of wanted to save it 'til later."

"So you've got something to look forward to?"

"Yeah," Michael smirked, "something like that. Have you had breakfast yet?"

"No, I'm not in the mood to go downstairs and wish people a merry Christmas in German."

"Let's get room service then."

"They could've at least sprung for some suites. Where are we supposed to eat?" Alex asked.

"In bed. What do you want?"

"You can decide for me. Just make sure there's strong coffee. And some juice. I want some juice."

Alex was in the bathroom when he heard Michael answer the door. Hearing it close, he waltzed out and stripped down to his underwear and a t–shirt, making himself comfortable in bed.

"Oh, so you expect me to bring it to you?" Michael asked.

"It's the least you can do seeing as you didn't get me a present."

"Here," Michael said, carefully setting the tray down on Alex's lap. "Can you hold mine for a sec?"

Michael kept his robe on and squeezed in under the sheets, carefully taking the tray back. "It's going well I think."

"What is?" Alex asked.

"The trip," Michael said, biting into a fried sausage.

"Mmm," Alex replied, sipping his coffee.

"Listen, you remember I had an idea for you a while back?"

"You've always got ideas. They usually involve me saying sorry or having to work more," Alex said.

"Yeah, I know. But this one doesn't require you to say sorry."

"Go on," Alex said.

"We're going to set up our own record label. You and me. Enough with working for those punks. They don't know what they're doing half the time."

"Sounds like a bit of a pipe dream," Alex said, chewing on his eggs.

"It's not. It's going to make us way more money."

"It's going to *cost* us a lot of money."

"It doesn't have to. I've got it all planned out. I've been speaking with lawyers and the accountants. I've done the research. Basically, you'll be able to record what you want. Even sign other artists."

"What? Like Prince does?" Alex asked, confused.

"Kind of."

"And you think we're up to it? That we could pull it off?"

"Never been more certain of anything in my life."

"I think I need to see numbers. Plans. I can't make a decision like that on the spot," Alex eventually said. He decided he wasn't as hungry as the kitchen staff thought he might be. He picked up the tray and carefully got out of the bed, setting the tray on the tiny table.

"You'd be an idiot if you did make a decision that quickly. When we get back to New York we'll go into it in more detail. Here, can you take mine as well? I'm done," Michael said, handing Alex his tray, which Alex set on top of his own.

For a moment Alex contemplated getting dressed and going back into his room. But seeing Michael, comfy and hirsute in his white dressing gown, made something stir inside. He turned around and got back into bed.

"Michael?"

"Yeah?"

"Are you ever going to find the balls to fuck me?" Alex asked, his adrenaline stirring him to life.

Michael's eyes widened. "Jesus Alex! You're my client. I've been trying to keep things professional."

"But is that what you want? For me to just be your client?"

Alex watched closely as Michael's chest heaved. Michael didn't seem to want to say anything, so Alex reached his hand out and snuck it into the gape of Michael's dressing gown.

"Because," Alex said, letting his fingers infiltrate Michael's briefs. "I want more than that," he added, squeezing Michael's appendage.

"There's no turning back if we do this Alex," Michael said, hardening under Alex's grip. "Like I've always said. All or nothing."

"I want it all," Alex said, thirstily. "Now!" he said, cozying up to Michael and tugging away at what he had in his hand.

***

They landed at Narita airport, greeted by the press and an awaiting throng of fans in the arrivals hall.

They didn't know it, but the Japanese label had organised (and paid) for fans to make their way out to the airport in an effort to build the perception of Alekzandr's appeal throughout the country.

Although Alex had already sold upwards of 300,000 records in Japan, he didn't have as high a level of visibility as many of his peers.

His Japanese label planned to change that with this visit, booking him solidly for TV shows, record signing appearances and an all–out press conference in the afternoon. Their goal was to make him as accessible to Japanese audiences as possible.

Ushered down to the conference room in their hotel where an assembly of forty or so journalists were waiting, Alex and Michael felt nervous. The idea that anyone could cotton on to their relationship panicked them, even if they'd only just been intimate together for the first time the day before.

Alex wore a lime green t-shirt under a military style jacket, his eyes lined by kohl. The press gave him a welcoming applause as he was ushered on stage and seated behind a linen covered table. Behind him, large blown up images of his record covers plastered the wall and slowly, a flock of cameramen and photographers converged before him, their flashes clicking away.

Despite the long flight, Alex felt reasonably fresh, and soon felt comfortable in front of the foreign press assembled before him. A pair of twin video screens on either side of the stage had finished playing some of his music videos and footage of his live appearance at the MTV awards, along with what now seemed like ancient footage of him from his whirlwind 1983 promotional gigs in Sydney and London.

As the MC spoke, Alex wondered if the journalists thought being in his presence that day was akin to being in an auto showroom where the new model being presented suddenly makes the previous one seem obsolete.

Their questions were respectful, concerned with filling in the details of his rise to his current position as one of the year's most exciting acts. He explained how his international background had shaped him and that he was proud of making music that wasn't much like anything else in the market even if his latest album wasn't receiving rave reviews.

Playing to the crowd, he reminisced about his time working in Japan and talked of his love for both traditional and modern Japanese culture, name dropping some of his preferred *enka* artists and some of the country's underground acts. By the end of the forty five minute session he felt he had absolutely won the group over, charming them with an uneven mix of humility, confidence, and a basic understanding of Japanese culture.

Afterwards, Michael and he were taken to dinner at one of Ginza's best restaurants by a label president, where they were joined by an executive of an electronics brand, who wanted Alex to front an advertising campaign for their products. Alex let Michael handle the negotiations but did his best to express his enthusiasm.

After dinner, the last of the day's appointments involved Alex giving an impromptu interview in the back of a stretch car for a popular nightlife broadcast. Michael was forced to sit up front with the driver while Alex played amicable guest to the inane interviewer and the camera man in back. By the time they made it back to the hotel after midnight, Michael crept into Alex's room and the two were dead to the world in seconds.

The following morning, they were taken to a photo studio near Shinjuku where one of Alex's heroes, Nobuyoshi Araki, was waiting for him (along with an army of assistants).

He did his best to befriend Araki, and together, they looked through the racks of clothes that had been assembled, Alex jettisoning some outright, taking just pieces of others, and meshing them with his own.

Surveying the combinations, Araki and he discussed the makeup and lighting, Alex remaining reverential but, as by now was the case, amply forthright with his own opinions.

Once make up was applied and a couple of test shots were run off, Araki took control of the shoot, and to the strains of The Cure, The Stalin and Shonen Knife, Alex resisted and assented to Araki's demands. Araki later told an assistant that Alex was more photogenic than attractive, but knew how to work his angles, the light and the costumes which had been supplied by Tadao, the hysterically funny designer who was also in attendance. The shoot ran past three in the afternoon, at which point Alex was ushered off to a television studio for more one on one interviews.

The next day there was yet more publicity to carry out and by then things began to feel mind numbingly repetitive. Another photo shoot, this time set around the streets of Tokyo was a more casual affair, Alex again mixing his own wardrobe with some of Tadao's clothes, before an in-store appearance in Shibuya kicked off mayhem, with hundreds of fans waiting for Alex outside a famous No Wave music store.

For the last two days of their Japanese stint, Alex and Michael were taken over to the Kansai. First up, was a day in Osaka to conduct a few radio interviews and another in-store appearance, this time in one of the city's sprawling department stores, where again, hundreds of young fans had lined up patiently all morning awaiting Alekzandr's arrival.

On the second day a trip to Kyoto was made, again for a photo shoot and a brief meeting with Suntory management, who were keen to sign Alex to one of their beer campaigns.

As with the electronics group deal, arrangements were made for Alex to return to Japan in March for filming and photography, the campaigns to hit the market in time for the summer of 1985.

For their final night in Japan, New Year's Eve, Alex and Michael were finally left to their own devices. Michael suggested they rug up and take a walk around the inner districts of the city, and find a lowkey bar to ring the new year in.

"There are times when I just want to be a normal person. I don't want be wined and dined," Michael said. "Besides, this city's full of 'em."

"Full of what?"

"Tiny bars. I'll have the concierge call ahead and book us a spot at one."

"I think this is going to be the quietest new year's I've ever had," Alex said.

"Do you want to do something else? I'm sure we can wrangle an invite to a party or something."

"No. I want to switch off tonight. Your plan sounds perfect."

***

After two days in Singapore for a meet and greet and a television appearance, Alex and Michael flew directly to Melbourne, where Alex's parents were nervously waiting in the VIP terminal.

Alex flippantly introduced Michael to his parents, who seemed a little older and less sprightly than he remembered, even if their voices were just the same.

On the drive back into the suburbs, Alex's parents asked about Athena and as he answered, Alex noted how attentive Michael was being.

Once Eleni and Michael had alighted from the car, Alex handed Oliviero an envelope despite his father's protests. Inside it was US$10,000 which was all that was left of Alex's last round of royalty payments.

There'd been changes at the house; a new wall and gate (to discourage fans who occasionally turned up unannounced) and a makeshift nursery for the new grandchild.

Alex's siblings joined them for lunch and they seemed happier to see him this time around, curious about his new apartment in New York and when he would let them visit.

In the early evening, Oliviero drove them into the city centre and dropped them off at the hotel where they had reservations for a junior suite. They quickly checked in and made their way up to their room on the 45th floor, whose skyline views proved of no interest to either, especially after a week in Asia.

They showered and, as they were now accustomed to doing, fell asleep the minute they hit the huge king size bed.

The following morning, Michael answered the door for room service, while Alex rifled through his bags in search of a package that he'd placed in there just days before.

"You know, I'm still offended that you never opened your Christmas present," Alex said.

Sitting at the table, he nonetheless presented Michael with another gift, a snow globe of Kyoto, onto the back of which Alex had scrawled a big love heart in felt pen. Michael looked up at him and smiled, caressing Alex's cheek. It was a corny gift.

Their working day kicked off at ten when an awaiting car shuttled them to the local record company offices where the local PR team gave the two a rundown of all the events planned over the next three days.

The mix of instore appearances, press and performances was working well. Sales of *Magic* had leaped in Europe, and Alex was finally out charting Athena again with *Just Us,* which was doing well everywhere (except in the US).

The tone of his interviews with the press in Australia was again different to that in Europe and Asia. Here, again in search of a local angle, many pressed him on the importance of his Australian identity and on his knowledge of his Australian peers, whom he'd been careful to study up on before touching down.

"I know my music is seen as a little too dance oriented here for the radio, but I think that's going to change now that there are all of these exciting bands popping up. Look at Eurogliders or I'm Talking. They're amazing! And then of course there's INXS who are changing everything. Michael Hutchence is fantastic."

Alex had received word that there'd been a volley of criticism in the Australian press, his label explaining that he and Hutchence were constantly being pitted against one another in the media, as if they were two competing saviours when there was only room for one. Hutchence, by virtue of his innate talents, was clearly winning the culture war in the press' eyes, while Alekzandr, they had it, was winning the commercial war.

In a Sydney television studio for an interview on *Sounds,* the presenter asked Alex to further comment on the rivalry.

"For me there is none. I've met him, I've seen him perform live and he captivates you. He's a one of a kind. But so am I. There's room for both of us. They're doing their thing, and I'm doing mine which is quite different. I think Australian music is maturing and I like the fact that we have different points of view. They deserve every success and I'm working hard to ensure I do too. It would be great if the media could just get behind the both of us rather than trying to create some friction."

The in-store appearance at Melbourne's Brashs store, then the country's largest music chain, drew a crowd of thousands, thanks in part to Alex's appearance on radio the night before. And though his appearance landed him a spot on the evening news, the narrative focused on how Australian radio was mostly ignoring Alekzandr's music, and how Australian music critics deemed him to be mere fodder in comparison to the richer, more diverse homegrown acts he was now sharing chart space with.

By the time Alex made it back into the television studios for two hugely popular shows he'd appeared on a year earlier, he was back on firmer ground. The hosts had welcomed him, congratulating him on his success, and commiserating with him about radio's ongoing disinterest in his work and the media's disparaging coverage of him.

"I just keep at it," Alex told the host of *Countdown.* "Radio will catch up. Times are changing. There's a generation of kids in this country who are sick of how radio treats them. They want some choices. People over fifty shouldn't be making the decisions for them," Alex said, smiling as the studio crowd (of teenagers) erupted in agreement.

Closing out the telecast with a performance of *Just Us,* Alex gave his all, flirting to camera and continually drawing out the excitement of the live audience.

Within a fortnight of his appearances, *Just Us* topped the Australian charts, thus becoming his first No.1 hit anywhere in the world. Propelled by all the promotional work, sales of *Magic* finally began to lift.

Landing in Mexico, an awaiting fax from Alex's label laid out an updated schedule. The Latin American promotional tour had been cancelled, the bulk of the interviews now to be done in Mexico City.

By the time Alex and Michael were back in New York, another single was released from the album to capitalize on the album's winning streak. Though it was a minor success, the *Broken Heart* single nonetheless generated yet more interest in the parent album.

After the intense promotional schedule, he mostly laid low over the new year.

In LA he auditioned for a series of films at Athena's urging, and spent weeks in talks with his record label and a touring organisation about his first American tour. In the Summer, he was called upon to perform *Dangerous* at the Live Aid event in Philadelphia, peeved Nik Kershaw and Howard Jones had been given longer slots than he had.

With the eventual release of *Dangerous*, in the summer of 1985, Alex returned to the headlines.

Its daring music video set off a firestorm as it hit the airwaves just as some of Alex's pre fame modelling shots surfaced.

In August 1985, some of the world's biggest selling tabloids published the tawdry images, in turn championing an effort to have Alekzandr written off as a *"perverted popportunist"*.

The sheer variety of images that the papers had sourced kept the gossip mill churning for weeks, the focus made worse by Alekzandr also receiving a special mention from the *Parents Mu-*

sic Resource Center even if they left him off their infamous *Filthy Fifteen* list.

Devastated by the blindside and humiliated by the phone calls from family and friends, Alex nonetheless put on a defiant public face.

Though a handful of female stars had fallen prey to similar scandals around the same time, Alex was determined to come out unscathed.

The controversy landed him his first proper primetime interview on *20/20*, where his arguments about the unauthorised publication of the pictures having stripped them of context fell on deaf ears. Nonetheless, he came across as articulated and self aware, criticising sections of the press that insisted the pictures were pornographic.

After the television appearance, sales of *Magic* surged, finally overtaking those of his debut, while *Dangerous* climbed to No.2, finally giving Alex a US top five hit.

But the controversy left his backers wary and prompted the scrapping of the Japanese endorsements and his planned North American tour.

As the intense summer drew to a close, Alex buckled down and began writing new material. Athena was in LA to film another movie, so the two made plans to meet in Australia at Christmas.

In the meantime, Alex was headed to Miami where a new chapter awaited him.

| 10 |

MIAMI

In 1985 Michael Estes bought himself an opulent house in Coconut Grove, Miami.

Initially it served as a trophy house, a belated present to himself after many fulfilling, if not incredibly lucrative years in the industry.

He'd bought it for a song from the widow of an old, notorious super–agent from the seventies, who, rumour had it, died in the pool room when his heart finally gave way after years of heavy drug use.

The house was part of Michael's fantasy screenplay about himself. One in which he practically pictured himself in a turtle-neck, riding out his early retirement by the pool or, on a boat (which was going to be his next major purchase).

But soon enough work commitments rendered the house less a dream home and more an unofficial headquarters for his and Alex's emerging, joint empire. Indeed, it seemed as if the villa was becoming a living temple to them both, filled with framed Warholesque portraits of Michael and dozens of Alex's gold and platinum plaques.

While Alex's second album was still in the charts, Alex began to focus on new material, keen to experiment with genres to expand his sound. To achieve this, he invited all kinds of producers and songwriters to the mansion to present or develop their ideas.

But Michael had plans of his own for Alex's music. He wanted Alex to make a leap towards a more mature, universal sound. It was part of his long-term goal to take Alex as mainstream as he could go. He wanted Alex's music everywhere; in the clubs, on the radio and filling out stadiums. In short, it was time for Alex to become a fully fledged pop act.

Michael had spent much of the year setting up Alex's new boutique record label *Kēvala* (a Hindi term for "solitary" or "pure"). He secured distribution of Kēvala's music through Alex's old record company, brokering a lucrative four album deal for Alex in the process.

Michael's own involvement in the deal put him in a position to be able to buy the Coconut Grove villa outright. He imagined that with Kēvala, they'd have their own 'Paisley Park' and as such, modelled the next phase of Alekzandr's career on that of Prince's.

Michael had lofty ambitions for Alex, desperate for Alex to be regarded as pop royalty but in the summer of 1985, Alex was still obsessed with low art. Namely, with Billy Idol.

Still playing the *Rebel Yell* album repeatedly, Alex's blind inspiration doomed many of the collaborations with songwriters in Coconut Grove, many of the songs sounding like inferior Billy Idol castoffs.

But as they settled into life in the Miami manor, Michael was contacted by an old friend; a Puerto Rican producer known to everyone as Rudy.

Rudy was an industry veteran who'd racked up dozens of songwriting and production credits across South America. Visiting Miami, where he had his own sizeable following, Rudy made it clear to Michael that he had a batch of songs that were perfect for Alex.

Where Rudy's typical songs were simple, catchy Latin pop affairs, the songs for Alex fit Michael's brief of being more sophisticated, with complex arrangements and only hints of Latin instrumentation.

Rudy's goal for his new material was straightforward. He wanted entry to the English speaking market, but he lacked an artist who could facilitate the shift.

Michael liked the songs. Though they were wildly different to anything Alex had recorded, with a bit of work, he was sure they were just the thing to widen Alex's horizons.

Alex and Ian had been trying new genres on for size in writing for the new album but hadn't yet found a clear objective for the new project.

In addition to their own *Idol* style songs, he and Ian had written a few songs that were a hybrid of pop and rock, and a couple of dance tracks composed on acoustic guitars as opposed to the Fairlight synthesizer they usually relied on.

Nothing earth shattering was coming out of their sessions, even if they were working on a sparse, electronic track with just a hint of guitar on it that Michael knew was going to be a winner.

But there was no consistency to Ian and Alex's music and nothing to suggest they'd found their sound. To Michael's ear, the Coconut Grove music was like a mixtape in dire need of direction.

Enter Rudy's songs.

With so much riding on their new venture, talk at Coconut Grove constantly revolved around the album. Endless conversations were being had about visuals, genres and possible collaborators. But eventually talk turned to the album's potential saviour, Rudy, whom Michael finally invited over.

Over the first of the many dinners they shared together, Michael watched as Alex and Rudy tentatively got to know each other. Rudy, already in his early forties, quickly found his mark with Alex (and Ian), regaling them with tales of the dozens of Latin super acts he had worked with throughout the sixties and seventies.

The boys hadn't really heard of many of the acts, but were intrigued nonetheless, impressed by the fact that Rudy was considered a living treasure just south of the border.

Rudy had a bulbous nose and leathery skin, but by all accounts, he also had a gorgeous Columbian wife with whom he was now living in Puerto Rico.

It took all but three dinners for the boys to fall under his spell and for them to lap up the invitation to hear some of the songs Rudy had in mind for their project.

As the music started, Michael watched as a hush came over the boys and they listened intently. Their reactions spoke volumes; raised eyebrows, tapping fingers, nodding, often in the space of the same instrumentation. Rudy played them five songs in total, the tape ending with some Spanish dialogue.

"I'm looking for someone to bring these to life for me," Rudy said, boldly looking Alex in the eye. "Someone to use them to tell stories. To take them into the world."

"That last one was amazing," Ian admitted.

Michael was sure he detected a hint of defeat in Ian's voice.

"All of them were," Ian added, "but that last one… it's like a journey."

"I love that one too. It was the last one to come to me," Rudy said. In fact," Rudy added, turning to Alex, "there's already two Mexican singers who are begging for it."

Alex looked at Michael for a moment, but Michael couldn't read Alex's mood.

"Rudy, I'm going to need some time. Can I hold onto the tape? Just for a week or so?"

"A week? What do you need all that time for?" Rudy guffawed, looking at Michael and winking with preternatural speed.

"I need that time to love them. To make them mine. I want to connect with them," Alex said.

"And what am I supposed to do in the meantime?" Rudy asked, smiling mischievously.

"Wait," Alex said. "Enjoy Miami."

For days, Alex and the tape were inseparable. Donning his headphones, he listened to it on a loop, spending whole days focusing on single instrumentals. With a legal pad and a pen in hand, he spent entire days consumed by the songs at the kitchen table, on the lawns and by the empty pool. He once even took to listening to the songs after a lovemaking session with Michael, much to Estes' chagrin.

But within a week, Alex was confident that he'd made the songs his own. He took the tape and his pad over to Ian's house and the two of them workshopped Alex's lyrics and his ideas for the vocals in detail.

Once Alex felt he had Ian's tacit approval, he instructed Michael to summon Rudy back to the property.

"Tell him we're using Ian's studio. It's ready to go."

"He won't go for that," Michael said. "He's expecting us to use the one in Westchester."

"Ian's is state of the art. It'll be better if we do the whole album in the one place."

"You know, you need to start thinking less about Ian's feelings and more about yourself," Michael said, nonetheless picking up the phone.

***

Rudy, Ian and Alex made a formidable team in the studio. Though Rudy's songs were impeccable, Ian and Alex worked hard to convince him that their tweaks would freshen up the sound and make it more contemporary.

Wary at first, Rudy came to see the boys as a team; Alex the creative director, Ian the techie capable of realising Alex's vision. Rudy was won over by their intense work ethic, surprised he could find no evidence to justify Michael's warning about their lack of diplomacy in the studio.

Alex referred to the project as *Miami Heat*, but its themes were anything but superfluous. Determined to "sing from the heart" and to craft his lyrics into something more substantial this time around, he dug deep, changing them as he went, going so far as to canvas opinions from anyone that came by the studio.

In the studio, Rudy pushed Alex in a way that Ian couldn't; as a singer. Time and again, Rudy forced Alex out of his comfort zone, patiently taking Alex through daily vocal warm ups and making Alex drink a concoction Rudy swore all Latin American recording artists swore by to keep their vocal pipes at their best.

Long before they finished up with Rudy, Billy Idol no longer seemed so vital, and Ian and Alex finally had firm ideas for their own compositions. Still, seeing Rudy off at the airport felt bittersweet.

"I was kind of hoping he'd stick around and play godfather for our songs," Ian said, watching Rudy walk towards the terminal.

"I know. But turns out his wife doesn't want him away any longer. The fucker left her at home with three kids," Alex said.

Returning to Coconut Grove after driving Ian home, Alex found Michael poring over a bunch of proofs he'd commissioned of Alex the week before.

"How'd they turn out?" Alex asked, opening the fridge.

"Not great," Michael said, watching him.

"What do you mean?" Alex asked, shutting the fridge door.

Michael looked at the photos again.

"What's wrong?"

"We can't use them. They're bad," Michael explained.

"The lighting?"

"No, it's not the lighting," Michael said, watching as Alex sipped at his beer.

"What is it then?"

Michael didn't say a word.

"Give me a look then," Alex said, putting his beer down on the table and snatching the loupe from Michael.

"Jesus, I look like shit! I'm so puffy!" Alex moaned, dragging the loupe from one still to another.

"We can't use them. Any of them," Michael added, desperately.

"Fuck Michael, why didn't you tell me? I'm all bloated."

"I hadn't noticed."

"How can you not notice? We're attached at the hip."

"I know," Michael said, "maybe I just like you with a bit of flesh, you know?"

"No, no, no! This is a disaster. What am I going to do?" Alex asked, throwing the loupe onto the table.

"Come here," Michael said.

Alex didn't budge an inch.

Michael raised his voice. "Come here, I said!"

Alex relented, walking over and leaning against him.

"We'll go on a health kick. Starting tomorrow. We'll get rid of everything in the cupboards. We'll go running too."

"Ah Jesus, I can't run."

"We'll do it together."

Alex grabbed his belly, squeezing it in anger.

"I like it. Drives me crazy actually," Michael said, running his finger around Alex's snail trail.

"That's not helpful."

"We'll start tomorrow. You've still got six weeks before you fly out."

"Easy for you to say. You're already a fucking Olympian."

"Listen, we'll think about it tomorrow," Michael said, taking Alex's hand. "But for now, let's go upstairs. I want to enjoy those extra pounds while I still can."

***

True to his word, Michael cleared out the larder and the fridge and dragged Alex, practically kicking and screaming around Peacock Park the next day.

When Alex's motivation began to plummet days into the new health regime, Michael organised for a personal trainer he'd heard of to take control of the situation.

Andrew, a red–haired, self confessed gym fanatic, arrived shortly after sunrise each morning at 7am, putting Alex through his paces with a morning warm up in Michael's atrium, a six mile run around Peacock Park and the foreshore and a warm down back at Michael's.

Chatty and inquisitive, for the first two weeks, most of Andrew's questions went unanswered because Alex was unable to jog and speak at the same time.

When rain hampered their morning runs, he refused to give Alex a free pass, instead dragging Alex into the gym where he worked, putting him through a light weights workout he'd specifically created for the popstar.

In the time leading up to Alex's return to Australia, Alex spent six mornings a week with Andrew, heading straight to Ian's afterwards to keep working on their tracks. Unaccustomed to such a gruelling schedule, for the first time in his adult life, Alex was in bed by ten every night, exhausted.

With recording completed on schedule, Alex organised for Jasper to fly down to Miami for an early Christmas celebration.

"How long has it been?" Alex asked, giving Jasper a long hug in the arrivals terminal and taking his suitcase for him.

"Nine months. And now I'm about to give birth to a shitty film that everybody is going to hate," Jasper said, following Alex out to the parked car.

"That bad?" Alex asked, putting the suitcase in the trunk.

"Is this yours?" Jasper asked, motioning to the car and lighting a cigarette.

"No, it's Michael's," Alex said, carefully closing the trunk.

"Are you still mooching off him?"

"I'm not mooching off anyone," Alex said. "I've just been too busy to think about getting my own car."

"What's gotten into you? You look all pale," Jasper added.

"I'm on a health kick. No booze, no food, no fun. I just got back from a run."

"Jesus, it doesn't look like it's doing you any good. You look like shit. That hair colour is no good on you. It makes you look even more washed out."

"Are you going to take your critical glasses off at some point today?" Alex asked.

"I will, but first, tell me. The fitness kick; was it your idea or Michael's?"

"His."

"I knew it!"

"I was looking like shit," Alex said, getting into the car.

"Bullshit," Jasper said, opening the passenger door, and slamming it behind him. "You were looking like yourself no doubt.

But it didn't fit into that 'world superstar' crap he's trying to make you into."

"It's not like that," Alex said, fastening his seatbelt. "I looked like a coke fiend."

"I've seen you as a coke fiend," Jasper said. "You pull it off. But seriously, you listen to him too much. Be yourself. It's what's gotten you to where you are. Don't buy into other people's ideas."

"Easy for you to say. You're behind the camera the whole time. Your face isn't splashed all over the place."

"It wasn't just your face that's been splashed all over the place, though, is it? You know I've got one of the scandalous photos of you pinned up on the wall in my office? The one with the dog."

"Fucking thing bit me that day. Seriously though? In your office?" Alex asked, checking his mirrors.

"Yep. My secretary was like, 'why you got a pimply arse white guy up on your wall?' I don't even cover it up when I've got meetings."

"You're a sicko," Alex said, turning on the ignition.

"Yeah, but you're my white boy. You don't even realise how much you stuck it to the man getting those pics published."

"I didn't have anything to do with it," Alex said.

"Yeah, well, the version of you in my imagination has always been more interesting than the real thing."

"Happy to see you too, you bastard," Alex said, pulling out of the VIP carpark.

***

Over dinner at Ian's, Alex savoured every bite of his meal while Jasper and Michael jostled for command over the conversation.

"I think he needs a new look," Michael said. "And everyone raves about Marcella. She's styling everyone."

"He doesn't need a stylist," Jasper countered. "But you're right Michael. Alex *has* changed, thank the lord. If we had to walk down the street together with him wearing those shitty Indian sacks or those leggings again, I'd probably shoot myself. But this goddam goth thing you've got going on," Jasper said, pointing at Alex, "it's all a bit much."

"Did the gay mafia order a hit on Alex tonight?" Ian asked, helping himself to a glass of wine, pouring one for Alex too.

"Yeah, when did the New York Post put you both on the payroll?" Alex said, miffed.

"Probably sometime between your second or third helpings," Jasper said, chuckling.

"I was hungry. I actually did stuff today. I didn't just loll around giving everyone my two cents worth like some people."

"Seriously though, when's the last time you went shopping?" Jasper asked. "And not at Goodwill, I mean."

"I don't know, Tokyo maybe? On my last day off. I hate shopping."

"Let's go tomorrow," Jasper said. "You need a day off anyway. Were you planning on going back to Australia looking like that? There'll be cameras pointing at you everywhere."

"No there won't. I haven't got anything new out at the moment. No one will care."

"About you, no. But Athena's movie is a smash. People are going to be watching her. And you as a result. Plus, you're going home to meet the family, and Alex, you've had that t–shirt ever since I've known you."

"I can't go shopping. We've got work to do," Alex said.

"No, don't look at me," Ian said, throwing his napkin onto the table. "I'm staying out of this."

"Come on it'll be fun," Jasper said. "Watching you spend money. I don't think I've ever really seen you do it."

"I wouldn't even know where to go. I've been holed up here this whole time."

"Michael?" Jasper said, sweetly. "Can we borrow the car to-morrow morning?"

"Sure," Michael replied, looking at Alex and smiling apolo-getically.

"See, he's a good guy," Jasper said, winking at Alex. "Now, who wants a joint? I brought some with me."

***

"We probably won't be able to speak while you're away," Michael said, in the car on the way to the airport.

"No," Alex agreed, taking a drag of his cigarette.

"I'm going to miss you," Michael added.

"Me too. I wish it was you that I was going there with."

"Probably good for us to have a bit of time apart anyway," Michael said, turning on his indicator and slowly turning. "I've been pushing you hard."

"I don't even know what I'm going to say to her when I see her," Alex said.

"I'm sure it'll be like you say it always is when you're with her. That that *other* you will kick in."

"I don't know if he still exists… not after all this time here," Alex confessed, butting out his cigarette.

"You'll be alright kid. Spare a thought for me. This time tomorrow I'll be pulling up outside my parents' house."

"I'd like to meet them one day. To come to Puerto Rico with you."

"Listen, the time in Australia will be over before you know it. Make the most of it. Make the most of being with Athena. You mean the world to her," Michael said pulling the car over. "Got everything?"

"Yep. It's all in my bag."

"Well, give me a kiss and I'll see you next month."

| 11 |

FELICIDAD

In the past, he'd met wives or stolen glimpses of them from afar, but this trip signified the first time in his adult life that Alex was going 'home' to meet the folks: the in laws.

Neither Athena or Alex had told their families that they were married. Both were terrified that something as simple as a mother's proud slip of the tongue was all it would take for their secret to make its way into the public.

They were happier being known as the pop couple more focused on their careers than on each other. The public seemed to like their ambition. Besides, it didn't seem warranted to publicly acknowledge their union. Admitting they were married would only trigger concern from loved ones about how little time they spent together.

For showbiz's hardest working couple, the trip 'home' amounted to their first holidays in over a year. Soon enough he'd be back on the promotional juggernaut and she'd be in the studio recording another album, this time for a major US label.

Stealing two days to themselves in one of Sydney's harbourfront hotels, each slowly unpeeled for the other, their conversations like professional debriefings. And though it took some effort to ignore the assembled press downstairs who lay in wait, Sydney seemed like another honeymoon to them.

They spent Christmas with Athena's family, who were incredibly gracious and welcoming of him, and together they drove up to Forster where her parents kept a summer house. After a few days taking in the coast and getting to know the family, Athena and he boarded a flight to Melbourne for a week with his family.

It was his second opportunity to see his nephew who had been born just over a year earlier, but what struck him most during his visit, was how Domenic and Sofia seemed to latch onto Athena. She seemed to represent something "normal" from his world despite her huge fame and success.

Athena had a little trouble bonding with them, but loved Alex's nephew, volunteering to hold him, play with him, feed or change him… whatever it took to extract herself from the tedious conversations with Alex's siblings.

She adored his parents though, and started to understand what he was on about those rare times he permitted himself to talk about his family with her.

In her view, he wasn't quite the black sheep he painted himself to be. Rather, he was just so different to his siblings that they simply didn't know how to relate to him, their attempts to rectify that comically falling flat.

But their time in Melbourne was more varied than it had been with her family, with all kinds of family and friends coming by to pay their respects and say hello.

What Alex hadn't told Athena was, that while in Miami, he'd closed on a real estate deal of his own. His Australian lawyer had secured him a coastal property on the west coast of Victoria, and after a few sticky days in the city, the family migrated to the property which his parents had overseen preparations for in his absence.

The sea air and the comfort of the expansive estate improved the family dynamic somewhat, and visiting at new year would become an almost annual tradition for the family.

Athena eventually headed back to Sydney to spend her last week with her family, while Alex and his family stayed put.

And just like that, with Athena out of the Garden state, Alex's priorities and thoughts switched. He fell back into his usual thought patterns but let on to nobody, instead biding his time.

Re–entering the States, he'd neither need nor time to continue the navel gazing. Michael put him back to work, and as soon as it always did, Alex's career took over, engulfing everything in the process.

A spate of listening presentations were organised for industry staff and the press in a handful of cities around the world, Alex attending those in Los Angeles, Mexico City and Tokyo.

Busy with interviews, promo and music videos for the album, Alex now felt like something of an old hand. Yet the new project felt so slick and streamlined when he considered the improvised way his first two albums had come to life.

Jasper had directed a video to the first North American single, *How Many People.* The video referenced Elio Petri's *A Quiet Place In The Country (Un Tranquillo Posto di Campagna)* and featured Alex recreating a scene where an almost naked Franco Nero was tied to a chair with coarse rope.

Elsewhere, the lead single was *Side By Side,* for which Jasper created another remarkable video, again inspired by a cult film. In it, slick choreography was intercut with scenes referencing iconic moments from Kōji Wakamatsu's *Ecstasy of the Angels (??? ??).*

The songs arrived in a blaze of publicity in late February 1986, Michael and the record label staff having devised a promotional blitz including another international promo tour.

The junket was also a way for Michael to finalise venues for the world tour which would kick off later in the year, giving Alekzandr his first chance at a full-scale live show. When Alex wasn't in meetings, he was busy with his friend Xavier, who he'd brought along in the role of publicist.

On release, the music videos created mini controversies, pushing the boundaries of what was acceptable for television at the time, their sexual and religious imagery generating hype for the new material.

When the singles went on sale, they exploded across the markets, the slower moving US singles market leading to both singles charting simultaneously.

With the flurry of press came the reviews for the album. The consensus was that *Felicidad,* (the title *Miami Heat* had been discarded at the last minute), was an event album which heralded a more sophisticated Alekzandr.

One reviewer noted the album contained "a string of obvious singles and enough good hooks and innovation to suggest Alekzandr's play for a wider audience would pay off." Other reviewers also commended the new pop turn, referring to it as "savvy" and "smart", labelling the album an "early contender for the year's best pop album."

Released on April 3, 1986, *Felicidad* shot up the charts.

Michael's promotional campaign had worked so well, that by the time the album's third single, *Thinking About You* – Alekzandr's first ballad – was released in July, *Felicidad* had already been to number one in 22 countries, with estimated sales of eight million.

Pandemonium ensued, the new music easily eclipsing the success of everything Alex had done before, opening doors to Hollywood's vanguard and the entertainment industry in the process, who finally began to see Alex as the real deal. Kicking off an unbroken run of top ten singles and a slew of gold and platinum awards, *Felicidad* elevated Alex into the big league.

"A walking, golden pop god," one journalist said, referring to Alex's new appearance; platinum blond, toned and every inch a star. Interest in the music and in Alex catapulted him out of B–grade pop and into every teen magazine, who wasted no time in labelling him the year's biggest heartthrob.

The varied sounds on *Felicidad* were also helping Alekzandr conquer radio. *Thinking About You,* which he had written for both Athena *and* Michael (though he never let on), was a hit as much on the strength of its music as it was for its risqué video. The video, depicting Alekzandr at the centre of a bisexual love triangle, intrigued and outraged audiences, causing yet more controversy. Despite the furore over the video's themes, *Thinking About You* became Alex's first worldwide No.1, briefly topping the US, UK and Australian charts simultaneously, going on to become one of the highest selling singles of the 1980s.

As his records sold by the truckload, Alex and Michael worked day and night to keep the momentum going. Whether in Alex's New York duplex or in Coconut Grove, they lived and breathed work at all hours, and during the headiest months of the album campaign, there was no escaping business talk, not even for a minute.

While Michael thrived in that setting, Alex longed for some reprieve or for a quick break. He felt like he was at the centre of a hurricane and at times struggled with the intense interest in him and his work.

A distraction only appeared at the peak of the album's success, when Alex and Michael were invited to spend a week on a private Pacific Island, by Max Thwaites, an industry magnate keen to acquire Kēvala.

While Michael and Max talked shop, Alex sought company in Max's boyfriend Jake, with whom he relaxed on a tiny beach near the property.

Tanned and relaxed, when Michael and Alex left the island, they returned to LA to announce the dates of Alex's world tour.

The show would kick off at year's end in Australia before snaking across the continents for most of 1987, the logistics of the show to be handled by Max's newly formed touring agency.

Auditions and rehearsals began in earnest in September in LA. The premise of the tour was simple; an energetic dance pop show which would draw from all three of Alekzandr's albums.

Because Ian was busy at work with other artists, Rudy was brought on board as the show's Musical Director. Jasper created a series of simplistic video backdrops for the show, while the choreography was devised by Miles, who, by then had accepted that his fate was to be Alekzandr's personal choreographer.

Over the space of five weeks, Alex spent his mornings with Rudy's band, reworking and rehearsing 18 of his songs for the show, before moving into the dance rehearsal space in the afternoons to work with Miles and the dancers.

After a brief stint in New York to attend to some business and to make an appearance at an AIDS benefit, Alex returned to LA in mid November, for the full dress rehearsals. The full stage was erected in a sports stadium, and the troupe was put through its paces for ten days before the entire production was packed up and shipped to Australia for the first leg of the tour.

Landing in Brisbane, the gravity of the show began to hit Alex. *Was he really going to do this? Was he going to pull it all off?*

Fans had been tipped off to his arrival, hundreds at the airport waiting for him. Rather than please or comfort him, their presence made him nervous.

In the car, Michael gave Alex an Alprazolam to help calm the nerves, before accompanying him to the Brisbane Entertainment Centre to inspect the venue where the tour would kick off.

Over the following days the final rehearsals and sound checks were carried out under intense media scrutiny, Alex increasingly anxious about everything.

He awoke on Thursday, December 4 with a bout of nervous stomach after a restless sleep. After a morning of violent vomiting, and being attended to by his new assistant Kōji, Alex asked Andrew, his personal trainer, to give him a full body massage to help calm him down. Later, in the afternoon, Alex did his vocal exercises and worked out in the hotel gym before being taken to the venue, but he struggled to rein in his competing emotions.

At the venue, adrenaline helped him get through the final preparations. Everyone in his inner circle promised him he just had to get through the first song before everything would be fine. Between intermittent trips to the toilet, Alex oversaw the final sound and light checks, much to the crew's amusement.

The tiny toilet cubicle in the Entertainment Centre was almost imprinted into his memory. He spent half the time in it crying, the other half laughing in embarrassment as Kōji faithfully waited outside the stall.

"Kōji, how the fuck am I going to pull this off if I keep shitting myself?"

"Just take an Imodium and have a really stiff drink before you go on," Kōji said.

"Where am I going to find an Imodium at this hour?"

"I've got some in my bag," Kōji said. "I'll get you one. And some more toilet paper. You've already flushed an entire rainforest today."

"And the drink?" Alex asked, hearing Kōji's footsteps.

"I have a bottle of vodka in my bag."

"God, where did we find you? And what *don't* you have in that bag?"

"Air freshener," Kōji replied, handing Alex a roll of toilet paper under the door. "Hurry up. We have to get you into your costume."

At 8.35pm, long after the support group had finished, and just as Alex was about to be hoisted onto the stage, his legs trembling, Kōji handed him the vodka bottle. "Hurry up and don't let Michael see you. He'll fire me."

"You're a life saver," Alex said, taking a quick swig then scrunching up his face and handing the bottle back to Kōji.

"You've got this," Kōji said.

Alex watched him walk away to the side of the stage. He adjusted his earpiece, steadied his leg with his hand, closed his eyes and took a deep breath, just as the crowd erupted impatiently.

He breathed again, and when he opened his eyes, he was on stage, the heat of the lights and the huge, shadowy audience before him overwhelming him.

The music had started, but the first line of the song had sailed past him, he failing to grasp and verbalise it. Panicked, he smiled, aware there was a camera trained on him, projecting his image onto the screens on either side of the stage.

Embarrassed, he shrugged and shouted "G'day Brisbane!" to the 10,000 plus crowd whose roar filled him.

Alex moved straight into the next line of the lyrics to catch up with the band. It took all his concentration to suppress the nerves debilitating him and to quash the sinking realisation that this was the first time he'd ever been in front of such a large, dedicated audience.

He'd previously participated in benefit concerts and televised live performances, but this was the first time that the enormity of his appeal lay before him. Worse still, it was in his homeland, so he felt a pressure to be at his best.

By the time he reached the chorus in the second song, he began to find his stride. Concentrating on his moves and the notes he was supposed to hit helped subdue some of the fear and gave him a feeling of control. By the time he stopped obsessing, he realised he'd already completed the first act of the show and had made it to the first interval, but one of his backing singers approached him, reminding him he needed to go backstage and change and that she and the band had the situation in hand.

In a daze he did so, but couldn't hear anything that Michael or his assistants were saying. Like a mannequin with a microphone in hand, he was quickly redressed and re–positioned, a hydraulic sending him back onto the stage.

"Oh my gosh Brisbane, I got lost in the moment. How are you tonight?" he yelled as he stepped away from the trap door, the crowd's rapturous response bringing another smile to his face.

"Forgive me for being so focused," he said, running his hand through his hair, "but it's like we're living a dream tonight. It's so fucking cool that we're all living it together."

He surveyed the crowd and greeted the different sections of the audience before launching into three more songs. At the end of the act, he introduced the members of his band and sat at the edge of the stage.

"I can't believe it's taken us so long to put this shindig together. But now that we're all here, I should just stop talking and get on with it right? Yes, you there in the front row agree with me. OK, well, let's do it… 3–2–1 go!"

Such was the intensity of the night, that for years after he wasn't able to recall anything in detail from the show without relying on the video footage or his staff to corroborate the facts.

The Sydney dates that followed went much the same, though with each show, Alex was able to regain his composure and control a little sooner, until it was just the first song that all but paralysed him.

Over four nights in Sydney, Alekzandr played to more than 50,000 fans, but the prospect of moving on to Melbourne brought his nervous stomach back.

Although friends and family had flown up for the Brisbane and Sydney shows, Alex announced a strict embargo on them coming backstage in Melbourne. The media focus which had already been strong, only intensified there as the press began to descend on the tour. Interest in Alex's music was at fever pitch, and his presence in Australasia saw record sales boom there.

In his Melbourne hotel room, Andrew, now on the tour payroll, took Alex through a number of meditation techniques in addition to the usual warm up routine.

Rudy passed by Alex's suite at midday to give him his daily update as musical director, a role he was relishing. Partnering with Alex and Michael had brought him huge windfalls.

"Were you out all night last night?" Rudy asked unsympathetically when Kōji finally allowed him in to see Alex.

"No. I was here. Sleeping."

"Well, you look like shit."

"Thanks."

"You're supposed to look like a dreamy pop star. Not Keith Richards. Are you sure you aren't taking something?"

"No! I can't help it. I'm nervous. I can't get past it. I thought I had put it behind me."

"You know what," Rudy said as he sat himself down on the sofa. "I'm gonna let you in on an old secret. Nobody tells you this shit. But Rudy's gonna tell you. When I first got into the biz I was the same. I used to have to perform, but only in front of a few hundred people every night. Probably not too different to how you started."

"Oh no, I was lucky if I had ten people in the audience back then Rudy. Don't fool yourself."

"Well, it doesn't matter if you have ten people or 10,000 people. Basically, your problem isn't that you're nervous. We all get nervous. Your problem is that you don't believe in yourself. You think you can't do it. So you can't. Simple as that."

Alex sat up and put down the clipboard that he'd been looking over.

"You should think of this as Alekzandr's show. Not yours. We work for him. He is the show. He has to deliver it like he did in rehearsals. He is the focused *chingado.* You… you are a bit like a *cevote.* That makes things harder. It's like torture for your mind that you're doing this. The minute you put that costume on, forget Alex. When they put the make up on you remember that you are *Alekzandr the Chingado.* Not *Alex the Cevote.* I don't care if your family is here. Or your friends. Or your old school teacher. That's you, you, you. But it's not your show. It's his, his, his. Get that into your head. And don't look at me like a *sangano.* You know what I am saying."

Alex nodded.

"Now, there's some changes we have to make to a couple of the songs. The band thinks..."

The first Melbourne show, smaller than those in Brisbane and Sydney on account of venue capacity, was the most intense he'd perform on the entire tour.

Getting dressed, he was hit with the usual shaky leg and nervous stomach, but remembering what Rudy said, he took to the stage like a boss. Like he was at war. Steely faced, he broke into his opening sequence and didn't say a word to the audience until the end of the first act when he flashed a huge smile in relief, its broadcast sending the audience into a frenzy. Smiling, he turned to Rudy, who, from behind his percussive instruments, simply nodded in acknowledgement.

Alex took advantage of the moment to gush over his hometown audience. If he still wasn't sure the audience was being won over by his song and dance act, then he knew they were his after a seven minute monologue. With it, he regaled them with titbits from his now long gone past and about the family and friends in the audience. He charmed his hometown, and in doing so, made some headway in wrestling with his anxiety about doing the show.

Once the Melbourne leg ended, he lifted the other embargo he'd had in place; that of Michael spending time with him in his hotel room; setting out to make up for lost time the minute they landed in Wellington.

The Australasian press lapped up the tour. Dailies, news bulletins and the general press devoted lead items and front page articles to the show. The commentary underlined that while the tour wasn't exactly the greatest show on earth, it was essentially the story of a local boy done good; one of the first home grown stars to take on the world.

The praise was almost always connected to acknowledgement of Alex's commercial success, and at the last of the Australian shows, the show was interrupted in the second interval so that he could be presented with a plaque commemorating the multi–platinum status of the *Felicidad* album, which had already produced three No.1 hits and sold over 500,000 units in the local market, making it one of the highest ever selling local albums.

That year, the local industry founded its national music association, and *Felicidad*, the year's second highest selling album domestically, and its top seller worldwide, was recognised with a Special Achievement award.

During his time in Australia, it seemed the entire country was talking about him. Journalists sought out old friends, colleagues… anyone who had some local connection to the newly minted global star. Newspaper articles tried to spell out Alekzandr's exploits, professional and personal, while correspondents cobbled together footage for the local version of 60 Minutes who were running a story on the elusive star.

Michael enjoined Alex to sit down with them for an exclusive, encouraging him to be mindful of the Tall Poppy syndrome.

Filmed during the Melbourne stint of the show, the interview was a puff piece designed to flesh out Alex's back story and his transformation from street urchin to pop icon.

All told, the tour and the huge promotional activity behind it, helped the album return to No.1 for the third time, just as Alex wound up the Australasian leg in Perth.

After a short Christmas break which Alex spent at his coastal estate, the tour resumed in Japan a week into the New Year. Four shows in Tokyo, three in Osaka and two in Fukuoka were all welcomed by more pandemonium. Two dates in Hong Kong at the Coliseum also followed as a trial of the market, both selling out.

Though some of the media's interest in the tour could be attributed to it being scheduled during a traditionally quiet time for concert tours, by the time the tour reached London, the critics began to make themselves heard.

In London for five shows, Alekzandr's quest for superstardom was not lost on the press. One writer drily noted that "he has won audiences over more with his knack for hooks and a well–timed double entendre than for any particularly notable skill." Another, for perhaps the most respected UK music journal, observed that "his onstage arsenal is still underdeveloped for someone who has been around for as long as he has." That said, comments like these were often tempered with acknowledgements of his dancing ability and his growing vocal prowess.

In the UK and Ireland for seventeen sold out shows, column after column debated Alekzandr's stage worthiness, but when the Fleet Street papers described the show as "amateur hour" or "a watered down Jackson show without the talent", Kōji would make a point of "forgetting" to deliver Alex his morning newspapers.

"I think you shouldn't read the press," Michael said massaging Alex's shoulders one morning, as Alex read the reviews in Dublin. "It's just making you tense. Just have fun with it. The fans love it. And the merchandise is doing even better than we could've imagined. That's a good sign babe. The critics are just doing their job. Their words fuel your fans."

Alex swatted Michael away and threw the paper down. "I need to come out the end of this having learned something."

"You won't learn about stagecraft by reading the reviews of newspaper columnists. You're doing great. You really are getting better and better for the most part."

"I won't learn about stagecraft by listening to my manager either. Where's Andrew anyway? He's late."

"Listen kid, why don't you take a morning off. Relax a little. Go out for lunch somewhere."

"I can't relax Michael. Not when there's a storm around me."

"You wait and see. Once we reach the continent, you're gonna love it."

| 12 |

I'M JUST DANCING

The shows in Western Europe were better received than those in the UK.

During his February 6 show in Hamburg, Alex felt it was his duty to pay tribute to pianist Liberace who had died two days earlier of pneumonia; a complication brought on by AIDS. Alex draped himself over a piano he'd had wheeled out onto the stage, and his keyboardist play Franz Liszt's *Liebesträume*, a piece that Liberace had popularised in the 1950s.

Alex sang over the piece, reworking a set of his old lyrics to fit in time with the number. When the music ended, Alekzandr spoke softly into his microphone. He personally had no feeling whatsoever for Liberace but wanted to make a statement.

"What you said hurt him very much, even if he cried all the way to the bank. You might think he was uncool. But remember that he did his best to pursue his dreams despite having to face the lynch mob. And there's nothing cooler than that. May we move on and remember to treat all people with kindness and dignity. We're all dreamers, and we all dream of love no matter how different it looks for some. Rest in peace Wladziu."

The comments caused a mini commotion throughout the German press, tapping into the discomfort surrounding the AIDS epidemic and putting the spotlight back onto Liberace's larger than life persona.

Tweaking of certain elements of the set list improved the flow of the show by the time it reached the Mediterranean countries where *Felicidad* and its fifth single were firmly lodged in the top five.

In mid–March after the final European dates in Barcelona, the crew descended downtown to an underground club where they partied throughout the night to celebrate the end of the third leg of the tour.

The following day, Alex and his support team shifted camp into the offices of a recording studio to begin recording for a new album project.

With Rudy presiding over production, and the tour band providing instrumentation, the tracks for four songs were recorded over a week long period.

With the stage equipment on its way back to North America and the tour to resume shortly, the next batch of songs was scheduled to be recorded during a break in Chicago. Each batch would be sent to Miami so that Ian could focus on post–production.

The hope was that the entire project would be ready for release in September right after the tour's final dates in Rio and Saõ Paolo.

With *Felicidad* more than a year old already, there had been talk of simply releasing previously unreleased demos and B sides but Alex point blank refused. Hence the long days recording in Barcelona.

Michael, doing his best to coordinate the recordings and carry out the preparation for the imminent US dates, was working even longer hours.

On the plane to Montreal, Alex woke him from his sleep.

"Michael. I think we're working too much, don't you? I mean, these last few months, we've barely had any time together. I don't know what's going through your head other than business. We had more than a week in Barcelona, your favourite city, and we didn't once go out for dinner or drinks. We didn't even take a walk anywhere."

"It's just a phase I'm sure," Michael replied, rubbing his eyes. "I feel like I close my eyes and I dream about all the things we have to do. It's endless, but the tour is going so well because it's all getting done."

"It's not sustainable. It's not healthy for us Michael."

"What are you saying?"

"I'm saying I bet you have no idea what is going on in my mind if it's not related to the show," Alex said, lowering his already hushed tone.

"Are we in trouble?" Michael asked, now alert.

"Michael, I'm gonna be honest. If we keep going at this pace, I'm going to be burnt out by the end of the tour. And not just professionally."

"Any suggestions?" Michael asked, gripping his armrest.

"Firstly, it's back to sleeping in the same room. Everyone on this tour knows about us anyway, who gives a shit? I want my life back. I signed up for a tour, not Sunday school."

"And if it leaks to the press or gets back to Athena?"

"We'll get adjoining suites, like we used to do. Frankly, right now I don't care who finds out," Alex said.

"You're just tired, you don't mean that. Think about Athena."

"If you'd been paying attention you would've noticed she and I have called things off. I think while we were in Holland. Jasper told me she's seeing an actor."

"And that doesn't bother you?" Michael asked.

"Why would it?" Alex asked.

Michael looked at him, confused.

"Neither of you are going to have it easy if the press finds out she's left you for a movie star. Who is he anyway?"

"One of the Brat packers."

"That doesn't exactly limit it down," Michael observed.

"It doesn't matter. I'm happy for her. She told me she needed some time to reassess. But Jasper told me the whole set is talking about how hot and heavy things are with them."

"And you're okay with it?"

"Of course I am. I'm not a hypocrite. Anyway, we have to do something about us before things get worse. And they will get worse, because there are way more shows to manage in the States than we've done so far. I'm going to get Kōji to be my go between with the band and the crew for now on. I don't want to spend two hours a day in meetings. I will give him my notes the night before and then he can check in with me after breakfast. I plan on taking back my mornings. What do you do in the mornings that you can delegate?"

"I do a million things in the mornings," Michael said.

"Well, you need to decide what you can ask someone else to do. Lighten your load. I want to wake up to you and have breakfast with you. Everything else can wait. We should have a proper tour manager anyway; you've done it long enough. I'm pretty sure we can afford it."

"I don't know where I will find someone soon enough to start with the next leg," Michael said.

"I've already found her for you. Her name is Celia. She's waiting for us in Montreal. She's great and she has worked with a million people before. I was thinking that if you like her enough, she could even become your assistant. You can't keep going at this pace. And, I won't accept it. You can't have it all and do it all."

"Are you firing me Alex?"

"On the contrary. I'm promoting you. You're my boyfriend again. You can decide how to divide up your responsibilities, but just think about the big picture. You have a client and a lover who is growing impatient and who is trying to do the right thing by you. I just want mornings and nights back. And I'm paying Celia, so you'll basically be getting paid to do less."

"Really? I mean, I feel like you're demoting me."

"Think smarter. I'm doing what I can to get our relationship through a rough patch. Think of it as a reward. I'm handing over a lot of my stuff to Kōji too. Delegation; it's my new favourite word. It's gonna be good for us. Besides, how were you planning on doing the show and overseeing the album as well? Are you nuts?"

"I don't know. I just figured I would work it out."

"You know, it'll be nice if we can see something together in all these seventy eight cities you're having me do shows in."

"Eighty one," Michael said.

"Eighty one what?"

"Eighty one cities. We added some more shows in Brazil."

"And you didn't bother telling me?" Alex asked.

"It's not that. I just didn't have the time," Michael confessed.

The North American leg of the tour kicked off in Montreal followed by dates in Toronto and Chicago, where Alex and the band resumed recording for the upcoming album.

There was talk of including a couple of the new songs into the set, if only to combat the boredom of performing the same songs on a nightly basis.

As the tour wound its way around the States and into Florida, Alex's focus shifted towards the new album.

A week workshopping and discussing the songs in Ian's studio confirmed Alex's fears. Many of the songs were just not up to scratch.

"I think we should bring someone in to remix them," Ian said. "Right now they all sound as if they were performed by a wedding band," he added.

"And you can't do it? Remix them?" Alex asked.

"I can try, but it would be better if we got someone else in to do it. I can talk to some people. But why don't you contact Vince? I reckon he'll be up for it."

"Vince? London Vince?" Alex asked.

"Yeah. Just tell him that we want to strip the band's sound a bit and to add some programming in. He'll be up for it."

"And the new songs that I've written? *Feel* and *I'm Just Dancing.* Do you think it's worth recording them?"

"May as well. If we need to, we can chop and change them around a bit if they sound too Rudy like," Ian said.

"Do you think I should say anything to Rudy?"

"No! Just go through with the last session in Houston. Get it done and we'll play around with whatever you come up with later."

Before leaving Ian's, Alex made two crude cassette copies of the demos and asked Ian for two FedEx bags.

Alex attached a post it note to one tape reading *"Need two treatments. Interested? –A."* and slipped it into one bag along with the details of the hotel he would be in in Mexico City.

Into the other bag, he placed a copy of some of the songs Ian had been working on from the sessions along with a handwritten note.

"Thank you for the last batch of remixes, they were wild.

We've been using your version of the songs for the show.

I know you're busy, but I need your help.

Listen to the tape, then tell me if you can put your stamp on it. All of it.

I feel like it needs a bit of a Vince touch to bring it to life, and anything you want to do with it, you have my approval to do so.

I'm attaching Kōji's contact details and our schedule. Leave word with him and I will get back to you personally.

–A."

When Alex arrived in Mexico City, there was an envelope waiting for him at the hotel. He recognised the handwriting and smiled, taking it up to his room with him. Opening the envelope on the bed, he looked at the post it note that was its only content and laughed.

"Kōji can you get me Jasper on the phone?"

"You are such a cunt!" Alex said when Jasper finally answered.

"Hola Mariposa. How's Mexico?" Jasper replied.

"Great. My hotel room is a hole though. And I'm literally over everyone. I'm so tired of seeing everyone's faces."

"Not Kōji's though, right?" Jasper asked.

"Oh no, I adore him. And Michael is back in the good books. He literally got me all worked up last night in Houston and he rocked my world."

"That is some majorly adolescent shit! How's his new assistant working out?"

"She's my new idol. Super–efficient, talks back to him, likes her drink and when she gets nervous she spills about her ex employer. Big things that nobody should ever know."

"Who's her ex employer?" Jasper asked.

"You and I were talking to him at the MTV awards."

"No way! Will she tell me everything when I meet her?"

"Because you're going to come down and do the one video? And not the other because quote, 'I can't have my name attached to something so embarrassingly primitive' end quote?"

"Yeah something like that. No seriously, I don't have time to do both, and yeah, I don't wanna be involved in that other one, but the first song is good. Is that still a demo? Anyway, I have a great idea for it. I could do it on a couple of handhelds, probably two days max. Maybe three days with some scenic shit, but for you, in and out in a day or two," Jasper explained.

"Um, do I get to hear about the idea?"

"Better if I come down and explain it in person. When can I come?"

"Well we are here for the next two weeks and then we are going to Argentina," Alex said tiredly.

"How long are you there for?" Jasper asked.

"A week. But we are only doing two shows. The mega shows."

"Ah, that's right. They're filming those aren't they? OK… if I come then, then maybe I can poach a couple of your camera guys?"

"Yep. Okay. I will get Kōji to organise stuff for you. Shall I have him call you tomorrow?" Alex asked.

"Yep. Going now. The Scot is back. He's in the living room watching a video. Love you homo."

"Love you too Lassie."

In Buenos Aires, playing to the biggest audiences of the tour, more than 80,000 people piled into the stadium for the first of two shows. In the down time between the shows, spaced two days apart, Jasper's idea for another risqué video came to life in black and white. In it, Alex, wearing a slightly transparent body costume, performed to camera, bending and contorting his body in choreography created by Miles. A second parallel sequence of the same routine was shot again in black and white, but this time with Alex completely naked. The sequence was reshot a third time, but in colour.

In Buenos Aires, Alex also received confirmation that Vince was already remixing the material. Alex decided to sit on the news until he was back in the States. No point spoiling the end of the tour for everyone, let alone his musical director.

When the final shows wound up in Brazil, Alex felt tremendous relief. Relief not only that the drudgery of daily touring was over, but that he'd be able to be back in New York and not be surrounded by the same faces every day.

Back in New York, Alex realised that the press had been humming with stories of his and Athena's split.

She'd left a message on his answering machine asking him to call the minute he was back. He procrastinated about calling her, preferring instead to first wind down from the flight with a nap.

In the evening he called her. He hadn't dialled the number since the night after his first show in Rotterdam.

"Hey," he said. "You okay?"

"Listen," she whispered, Alex hearing a male voice in the background, "I'll call you back tomorrow okay? I'm fine, there's just all this nonsense in the papers and some people panicking."

"Should I be worried?" Alex asked.

"No, I swear, I'm fine," she promised.

"Just call me if you need me. Doesn't matter what time."

He'd taken an Ambien after speaking with Athena and didn't wake until after five in the afternoon when he heard someone entering the apartment. Groggily he called out and was shocked to hear the response.

"It's me," she said. "Were you sleeping?"

She was now at his bedroom door.

"What are you doing here?" he asked, sitting up in bed and straightening up his hair.

"I figured we should talk in person," she said.

Alex stretched and yawned.

"Can you put a coffee on?" he asked, kicking his legs out of bed and pulling on the grey trackpants that were on the floor.

Shuffling into the kitchen shortly after, he gave Athena a hug.

"Did you get the red eye?" he asked.

"No, I flew out at seven this morning. Came straight from the airport."

"Are you okay? You had me worried on the phone," he said.

"It's fine," she said, pouring his coffee into a mug.

"You're not having one?" he asked, taking the mug.

"I won't sleep if I do," she said.

"So, is it true?" he asked, blowing on his cup.

"About as true as you and Michael," she said, tucking her hair behind her ear.

"So what are we going to do?" he asked, moving over to the table and taking a seat. He was tempted by the fruit in the bowl but decided against it.

"Well, it's not serious. With Robert, I mean," Athena said, pulling out her cigarettes.

"Does he know that?" Alex asked.

"He wants it to be serious. Wants to get married."

"Ah," Alex said, sitting back in his chair. "And you don't want to?"

"I'm already married. Remember?"

"How long have you known? About Michael I mean."

"Since Christmas in Australia. You were a completely different person. I put two and two together."

"So what do you propose we do?" Alex asked.

"I've been thinking. We've both put a lot of money aside. Neither of us needs to work any longer. We could just walk away from everything. See out our obligations. Move back to Australia. I think I've had enough."

"No, seriously, what did you have in mind?" Alex asked.

"I'm serious. No more living out of suitcases and traveling endlessly. Not for work at least. You see out your commitments, I'll see out mine. And no more Michael, no more Robert," Athena said.

"Athena, I don't think it's as simple as that."

"But it can be. I mean, I've been thinking about it. I can turn a blind eye to some things. I don't have a problem with that at all. But I don't think we can keep going. Never being in the same place at the same time… I don't think I want to do this anymore."

"Oh babe," Alex said, taking one of her cigarettes and her lighter. "I don't think I can just walk away. Don't think I want to," Alex said. "Not after all the effort it took to get here."

"But I've been thinking about that too. You could write for other people. Produce. You were miserable touring day in day out. Look at you, you're a wreck," Athena added.

"I literally just got back. Of course I'm knackered. But it's what I signed up for."

"And us? You also signed up for us too," she said. "Things could be however we want them to be. We can even have a couple of kids if we get out while everything's still good."

"Babe, is it possible that you're just feeling overwhelmed? That you need a break? We could go somewhere. Or just hang out here. Everything else can wait for a bit."

"I think I'm done with waiting Alex. I think we have to make a radical change. I know it doesn't sound logical, but it would be the best thing. For both of us."

"Listen, unpack your things. We'll cook up some dinner and have a night in tonight. Unplug the phone. Just you and me."

"Alex, I want you to take me seriously."

"I am taking you seriously," he said, standing up and taking his cup over to the sink. "I think you're right. We need to spend a bit of time together," he continued. "Let's not make any rash decisions in the meantime. Let's spend a bit of time together and work things out. Work out what's best for the both of us."

"I have to be back in LA by the end of the weekend," she said.

"Well, if you can't move things then we'll just have to make do with the time we've got. Go unpack your things, have a shower. I'll see about organising dinner."

Later that week he pulled a few strings to secure an appointment with a renowned couples therapist. He figured he owed Athena at least some form of effort, regardless of whether it was sincere or not.

Athena explained her views to the therapist and was asked to put forward her best and worst case scenarios. Alex let her speak without interruption, and smiled and laughed along with her at all the right times.

"My best case scenario would be that in ten years' time we're still married, still great friends and there are no hard feelings about what we left behind," she said.

He smiled benignly as she spoke: he hoped that it was clear on some level that he absolutely adored her.

"My worst case scenario is that we don't reach an agreement and we continue in this way where we are just pursuing our own lives and we're just a couple on paper," Athena added.

She held it together, and the therapist, content that Athena had been clear with her positions, asked Alex to verbalise his.

"I have to say that I love and admire Athena. She has always been more rational than me. And when we agreed to get married it was almost like a pinkies pact you know? It just seemed like it would be a great thing for two friends and lovers to do. And I think we can both acknowledge that it wasn't ever a traditional decision at any point. And because of that, we've treated the whole thing quite flippantly. Just as we prioritised everything else when we went through with it, it's been at the very bottom of both of our agendas since."

Alex looked at Athena and at the therapist who had a fixed poker face.

"Now, because things are a bit pear shaped, Athena thinks the alternative is to completely flip things. To abandon everything we've worked for. And for me, as much as I love Athena, I don't think I should burn everything down just because she's prepared to."

"So, what are your best and worse case scenarios?" the therapist asked, raising her voice slightly in an attempt to stop Athena from interrupting.

Alex looked at Athena and then at the therapist.

"In the best case scenario we'll find a balance where we don't have to give up on anything. Maybe just make some compromises here and there. In the worst case scenario, I'll end up having to give up everything we both believed in and I'll be reduced to being her security blanket. I'll become a dad because we'll be forced to work towards Athena's mental list of what life should look like because she's changed her mind."

"But I view our marriage as something serious Alex. Don't you?" Athena asked, her alarm evident to all.

"I think our marriage is about our bond. It's never been about a daily living arrangement or a shared project. I just think you're making it into something it's never been because you're a bit burnt out."

"It's not fair that you're painting me as some crazy person who is having a breakdown. That's not what's happening here. You're right, our marriage has never been conventional but you don't agree to marry someone if you don't intend to have that person be a major part of your life."

"In fairness, I don't think Alex is saying that," the therapist said. "But how do you respond to what Alex is saying? That basically you are suggesting something that is radical compared to what you both currently have?"

"I know it's big. I know it's a huge change that I'm suggesting. But we've always been unconventional. I'm just saying that for us to go forward we have to make sacrifices. I'm not saying we have to have kids tomorrow. Or that we have to move to Australia next week. The work we do is not going to last forever, and I don't think he can see that. I think we have to start thinking about what life is going to look like after this all evaporates. Because it will."

Alex looked around the room. It was the first time he'd been in a therapist's office. It looked much like he imagined one should look, full of books, diplomas and expensive furniture.

"It could disappear, like you say. But it might not. And if it doesn't, what do we do then? I'm not prepared to give up on what I've spent my whole life working for. I don't think I'd be able to look you in the eye knowing that you forced me to give up on my dreams because we naively agreed to something without really thinking things through."

As Athena's body language stiffened, Alex saw that the therapist was carefully watching him.

"I can't believe you're being so flippant about it. It's like an inconvenience to you," Athena said. "It's like I no longer factor into your decisions. That I don't matter to you anymore," she said, shaking her head in disbelief.

They sat in silence for a few moments and just as the therapist was about to break the silence, Alex decided to speak.

"I just don't see both of us being happy if we suddenly pursue our marriage like a Plan A instead of the Plan B it's always been."

"Jesus, Alex," Athena said, clearly exasperated.

"Alex, it sounds like you've already made up your mind."

"Exactly, that's the problem," Athena said.

"It's not that. It's just that if Athena insists on changing our arrangement, then it's a new arrangement. And I didn't sign up for that."

"So, it's status quo or nothing. Talk about ultimatums," Athena sniped.

"I won't give up everything Athena. I won't start stepping back from everything I've invested myself in to pursue something that won't make me happy. You shouldn't ask me to. If you're prepared to compromise, I am. If more of the same in a more healthy way is not good enough for you, then we should just leave it while it's still good between us. You know?"

"I don't think it's good between us Alex. Not if we've reached this point."

"It is good between us Athena. Because in our own ways I think we're both still trying to look out for each other. Me sitting here saying it's a disaster in the making is as much for your own good as it is for mine."

"Well, I guess that's it then," Athena said, beginning to put on her jacket. "I mean we could waste time booking more of these sessions, but we would probably be better off just booking time with some divorce lawyers instead."

"Alex, Athena, I think the two of you need a bit of time to just cool down. This is just the beginning of the conversation that the two of you should be having. Not the beginning and end."

Athena looked at Alex and smiled and then looked at the therapist.

"No. We're good. We'll always be each other's firsts."

Athena straightened up her hair and looked over at Alex.

"I'm going to need some time to cool off. I'm going back to the apartment to get my things and then I'm going back to LA. I'll call you once I've spoken to some lawyers."

"Are you sure? Let's you and I talk about things tonight. You can get your flight tomorrow. I don't want you going back to LA with things like this."

"Bye Alex. Thank you, doctor," Athena said, opening the door and walking confidently out into the reception towards the lift.

"Before we end things, I just want to say that you do come across as incredibly flippant, despite your reasons," the therapist said. "You may want to take that on board if you ever find yourself in another meaningful relationship. That is, if you are not already in one."

"You take AMEX, right?" Alex asked, flicking his credit card onto the therapist's desk.

***

Feel was released in September and created a storm of controversy for its suggestive lyrics and the racy videos which Jasper and his team of editors had to create; one version for late night play, the other more suitable for general viewing.

When what Alex referred to as the cash–in album, *I'm Just Dancing,* arrived in October, it became his fastest selling album to that date, clocking up sales of six million by year's end. Sales continued into the new year, spurred by the success of the titular second single.

Felicidad wound up its chart run around the same time, with sixteen million sales worldwide, and its eventual catalogue sales topped twenty million, making it Alex's biggest ever selling studio album.

Aside from a limited promotional campaign, spearheaded out of New York and an appearance at the MTV Video music awards, where he walked away with two trophies, Alex kept a low profile for the remainder of the year, exhausted after having been on the go for more than two years and struck with feelings of guilt over how things had ended so coldly with Athena.

He split his time between New York and Coconut Grove. Though *I'm Just Dancing* was selling well of its own accord, Alex realised that he just didn't have it in him to get out and promote his work as he had always been prepared to do in the past.

Instead, to put the mammoth two year pop icon project behind him, in December 1987, Alex dyed his hair back to its natural dark tone and made it clear to Michael that he was taking a sabbatical.

Any time Michael so much as broached an even remotely career oriented topic, Alex reminded him of the new "appointment clause" in their relationship where business talk was only permitted at pre–agreed times.

Even dreams have limits, he thought. It was now time to focus on his personal life and enjoy some of the breathing space that two years of relentless effort had earnt him.

| 13 |

NEW YORK

"It's turning out to be my divorce album isn't it?" Alex asked rhetorically, in one of the few moments that he managed to keep it together in the studio in October 1988.

Ian looked at him, trying to work out which one Alex was referring to. The last year had felt like a series of collateral divorces; romantic, personal and business separations that had messily overlapped and reshaped Alex's intimate circle.

All Ian, and Peter, Ian's new assistant, knew, was that it was a miracle they were nearing completion of the album. Especially after so many working days lost to the chaos the upheavals brought.

At first, they thought all the phone calls Alex was taking in the corridor were with Michael. They'd start out innocuous enough but would eventually reduce Alex to hysterics. With so much to do in so little time, Ian and Peter had no choice but to ignore the distraction and work around the chaos.

It had seemed more than reasonable when, exhausted by his world tour, Alex announced he was taking a sabbatical. He hadn't given anyone a timeline but made it clear that he would only return to his music when he felt ready.

That had set off a chain of events and a huge change in everybody's dynamic with Michael.

At first it lingered in the tension that could be felt in his and Alex's conversations. Though it was awkward, everybody tried to ignore it, dismissing their arguments as the kind any tired, overworked couple gets into, the tension evaporating before the cycle gradually began again.

But at some point, the cycle came to an end, with Alex's decision to leave Coconut Grove. At the height of an argument, he packed up his belongings and called himself a taxi to the airport, leaving Michael reeling.

With Alex back in New York, Ian constantly found Michael at his door, imploring Ian to go to New York and convince Alex to return.

"I can't ask Jasper or Xavier to do it. They'll just laugh in my face," Michael had said at Ian's front door.

Ian remembered that night vividly, because the doorbell had rung after he'd settled in on the couch, ready to finally watch *Back to the Future* on his newly purchased video recorder.

"Maybe you should just give him a bit of space," Ian said, unwilling to let Michael in, lest Michael commandeer his entire evening. "Maybe not make such a big production number about him wanting to have a break. Seems more than fair to me that he wants to kick back a bit and relax. Maybe it's a good chance for us all to concentrate on our own stuff."

Michael left that night, but it seemed he left unconvinced. Each time he returned to Ian's door, Ian's pity for him grew.

In time Ian relented and let Michael in, listening to Michael who couldn't understand why Alex still wasn't taking his calls. He'd considered every option; calling daily, giving Alex space… even going to New York himself to break down Alex's door. But Michael just didn't know what to do without the counsel of Alex's closest friends. After a month of Michael's regular visits, Ian relented, calling Alex in New York, warning him that he was coming to visit.

It was April and Ian recalled finding Alex's long, wooden table covered in legal documents and Alex in grime. Alex gave him a hug and told him to help himself to a beer before heading into his loungeroom.

Opening his beer, Ian couldn't resist peeking at the documents. There were all kinds of contracts sprawled out over the table; some pertaining to Alex's properties (the duplex, the beach house in Australia, and it seemed, houses in London and LA). There were even documents regarding Alex's holdings in Kēvala and his contractual obligations to it. But it was another set of documents that knocked Ian for a six.

"Alex. Can you come in here for a minute?"

"What?" Alex asked, walking over and leaning over one of the metal chairs at the table, looking at the table as if he was expected to see something out of place.

"You're getting divorced? From Athena?"

"Oh yeah," Alex said, absentmindedly.

"You didn't tell me you were married in the first place."

"I couldn't," Alex said.

"Why not?" Ian asked.

"Because we promised each other we wouldn't breathe a word of it to anyone. Not to Michael. Not even to our families."

"Jesus!"

"Don't get all offended," Alex said, scratching the back of his neck. "I am entitled to keep some things to myself. Even from you."

"What's with all the other contracts?" Ian continued, frustrated by Alex's coldness. "You having a fire sale?"

"Ha! The divorce lawyers needed them."

"Is she taking you to the cleaners?" Ian asked.

"No. Quite the opposite. We sat down and looked at how we could both walk away with equal shares of our assets."

"No shit?" Ian said, flicking through the separation agreement.

"I owed her that much. Even if she's probably got more money than I have."

"What's she getting?" Ian asked, putting the papers back.

"The house in LA. I never wanted it anyway."

"I didn't realise you even had one," Ian quipped.

"Bought it on the off chance I ended up in LA. Seeing as I have no plans of ever living there, I figured, who cares, you know?"

"Listen Alex, it's still light out. Shall we go for a walk somewhere? Get some fresh air? When was the last time you left the house?"

"A few days ago, I think," Alex said, sniffing his armpit.

"Go have a shower, we can go grab a drink or a bite to eat. It'll do you some good."

Ian busied himself with tidying up while Alex spent a half hour in the bathroom. When Alex returned, freshly shaven and smelling clean, Ian felt he recognised his oldest friend again.

They headed to an old bar they used to love when they both lived in New York. But times had changed, and the once run-down bar was now an upmarket establishment with a VIP area that they were quickly ushered into.

"Listen, Michael is a wreck. He keeps turning up at my place bawling his eyes out," Ian said, scoping out the clientele.

"I'm sorry for that," Alex said, sipping on his drink.

"You're going to have to talk to him at some point."

"I don't think I can anymore. I don't know him anymore."

"What do you mean?" Ian asked.

"He's obsessed. Money. Contracts. Success. I can't remember the last time I had a normal conversation with him. We always end up talking about work."

"Well, he's worse now than when you left him, that's for sure."

"Ever since I stopped and he found out I was married, he has treated me differently. Doesn't see me as his golden goose anymore."

"I just saw him yesterday, Alex. He's devastated."

"I've put four albums out in five years Ian, and he's still banging on about making another one already. Left me a message on my answering machine just a couple of days ago. The last one nearly killed me with all the touring and everything else. I'm still not sleeping properly. I've got no libido and I just have no energy for anything. I just want to crawl up and die. Or sleep at least."

Ian studied Alex closely. He couldn't remember seeing him on the brink of tears like he was now.

"You need to find a healthier way of dealing with all of this Alex. It's not good for you. I felt like I walked into a squat when I got to yours tonight. All that was missing was the smell of piss in the hallway."

"I sent the cleaning lady home last week," Alex said, smiling wryly as he took a handful of peanuts. "She told me that she was sick of me being in the house, so I just snapped."

"You need to get your shit in order. Why don't you fly Andrew up? Get him to put you on a bit of a schedule? You love running."

"I hate running Ian. And I hate people that go running."

"Get real, I used to see you sometimes in Peacock Park. You had that dopey face that people that go running have."

"Get fucked, I did not!" Alex said, throwing a peanut at him.

"You did. The same dopey face you always get when you're around Michael. All that endorphin shit."

"Yeah, well, things change," Alex said, shifting in his seat.

"Listen, I'm not saying you need to get back to work or that you should come back to Miami. But you can't shut everyone out. Michael included."

"I'm not trying to shut anyone out," Alex said.

"Then what's going on? I've never seen you like this. And it really worries me."

"I don't know what's going on," Alex said, sighing. "I honestly don't. I thought, especially when everything went down with Athena the way it did, that I had everything under control. I was such a cunt to her about everything. I made a big song and dance about how she needed to find a balance in her life. She was talking about giving everything up and of us moving back to Australia."

"And you would've done that? With her?"

"No, fuck no," Alex said, shaking his head. "I thought I had it all worked out. I had Michael. I had a plan. I brought on staff. We were going to smell the roses for a bit. You know? I figured that I deserved that. That Michael did too."

"But?"

"But then I realised I had it all wrong, and that Athena in the end was the one who had worked it all out."

"What do you mean?"

"She saw through everything. We were married, but we weren't really a couple. But now I understand that it was the right marriage for the both of us. Because at the end of the day it's about knowing that someone's got your back. That they're not there with you because they want to make money with you."

Ian's mind raced as it tried to join all the dots.

"Listen, Michael can be a jerk, but I don't think it's a money thing with him. I think he's invested so much of himself in you and your career that he just doesn't know what to do with himself. He's got no idea now what to do with his time. He seems lost. Especially without you there."

Alex leaned back and put his hands on the back of his head. Ian felt the frustration.

"I... I just need to have some fun again. With Michael it's just work, work, work. I don't even think I'm attracted to him anymore."

Ian took a deep, nasally breath.

"Yeah well, you can't leave him high and dry like you have. Whatever you decide, you still have to work with him."

"Therein lies the problem," Alex said, waving the waitress over.

"Let him come to New York at least. Spend a day with him. Talk to him."

"Yeah, I don't know," Alex said. "I'm at the point where I wouldn't know what to say."

On Ian's return to Miami, Alex gave up the hermit act.

In the early spring at an A list party that a friend was hosting, he ran into Ferris, an old acquaintance. He'd known Ferris ever since his early New York days. Back then, Ferris had been a constant on the party circuit, and as Alex ascended the pop music ranks, Ferris worked his own way up, becoming one of the country's most successful creative directors.

Quickly, the two rekindled the friendship, hamming it up together at opening nights and parties across Manhattan.

Ferris made Alex his pet project for the spring, introducing Alex to a new world of people: film makers, modern day troubadours… artists and writers who Ferris pointed out were *real* artists. They were part of a New York scene Alex barely recognised.

Ferris both loved and loathed how Alex was such a consummate pop artist. During his substance fuelled monologues, he'd tell Alex that he wanted to mentor him and get him away from singing inane pop songs and co–opting old Hollywood imagery.

Alex and Ferris hit Manhattan three, if not four times a week, their good cop/bad cop schtick often spilling over into the city's gossip rags. At times they were joined by Jasper or Xavier, but mostly, Ferris dragged along a bevy of model/actors with whom he flirted outrageously.

Ferris' antics didn't bother Alex much. He was so caught up in having a good time and enjoying New York for the first time in years that he even tolerated Ferris' ham-fisted attempts at seduction.

Lines were only crossed at a party at Ferris' penthouse where a few dozen, reasonably well known guests were in attendance. Alex had come with Xavier, who made his excuses and left once the dinner party shifted outside to the deck.

"Promise me you won't get wasted," Xavier said, kissing Alex on the cheeks.

"I'll be good, I promise," Alex said.

"By the way, that printmaker guy has been staring at you all night. You should go for it," Xavier said, hugging Alex and making his way out of the party.

Alex clocked the artist and walked right up to him on the deck.

"Hey, I'm Alex," he said.

"I know who you are! I'm Akio, but everyone calls me Aki," Aki said, holding out his hand.

Alex admired its deep tawny tone and shook it.

"Why haven't I seen you around?" Alex asked, noticing that Aki had two different coloured eyes.

"I don't usually come to Ferris' parties. They always end up in tears," Aki said, smiling and revealing a dimple on his left cheek.

"Yours?" Alex asked, looking him over. Aki was taller than he was, but Alex noted they both had similarly stocky builds.

"No. How good a friend are you of Ferris'?" Aki asked, conspiratorially.

"Good enough, I guess," Alex said, "I've known him forever."

"So, you know what he can be like."

"Then why come if you're not a huge fan?"

"I was hoping I'd run into you," Aki said, smiling again. "You guys have been all over the papers lately."

"Bingo! You've run into me," Alex smiled, somewhat flirtatiously. "So now what?"

Aki kissed Alex on the lips, grabbing Alex's belt buckle and pushing his knuckles into Alex's abdomen as he plunged his tongue into Alex's mouth.

"I've been wanting to do that all night," Aki said, when he was done.

"Had I have known, I would've introduced myself earlier," Alex replied, pressing his lips together and running his tongue over them.

"I see you two have met," a voice boomed behind them.

"Tears," Aki said, raising his eyebrow and winking at Alex.

"We have," Alex said, curtseying as Ferris joined them.

"Do I get one of those? Kisses, I mean," Ferris said, a little sharply at Aki.

"Of course," Aki said, almost smiling, and then leaning in to give Ferris two air kisses.

"Alex, you know that MOMA has just picked up some of Aki's work?"

"I didn't know," Alex said. "We didn't get the chance to talk."

"We can continue our conversation in a bit," Aki said. "I'm going to get a drink. Do you want anything?" he said, winking at Alex's refusal and heading off towards the bar.

"You know he's like New York's motormouth?" Ferris said, brushing the hair out of Alex's eyes.

"Meaning he gives the best head in town?" Alex asked, readjusting his fringe.

"Meaning if he gives you head, everyone will hear about it," Ferris replied. "Be careful with him."

"There's a lot of people here tonight," Alex said. "Do you have the same mixed feelings about them?"

"I'm of half a mind to send everyone packing," Ferris said, inching a little closer to Alex.

"Do you have a light?" Alex asked, unflinchingly sticking a cigarette into his mouth as Ferris crowded him. Ferris lit Alex's cigarette with one hand and stuck the other in between Alex's legs, rubbing away.

"Ferris?" Alex said, looking him in the eye, blowing smoke into his face.

"What?" Ferris replied, rubbing Alex's balls even harder.

"Can you get your hand out of my crotch?"

"Why? You not enjoying it?"

"I am. But I only perform for audiences on stage."

"Do you want me to send everyone home then?"

"No," Alex said, licking his lips and boldly looking Ferris in the eye. "I just want you to take your hand out of my crotch."

"Okay, okay, don't get shirty," Ferris said, holding his hands up in surrender and shaking them, jazz hands style. "You're so coy when it suits you," Ferris added.

"Rufus is calling you," Alex said, gesturing into the distance.

"Probably wants to do a line. I better go see what he wants. We're rain checking what you just started," Ferris said, kissing him on the cheek and taking one last swipe at Alex's crotch.

An hour or so later, Alex made sure he timed his exit so that Ferris would see he was leaving the party with Aki, blowing Ferris a kiss as he got into the lift.

Though Ferris and Alex had made a point of seeking out fun and rowdy engagements during the spring, when an invitation to a black–tie event in Connecticut arrived in the mail, Alex knew he was obliged to attend.

The president of his parent recording label was throwing a birthday bash and Alex was aghast at the handwritten note the president included in the envelope. It sought assurance that both Alex and Michael would be in attendance, he not having seen or heard from either of them in months.

The importance of the event necessitated a truce in hostilities, so the night before the party, Alex called Michael's New York number after the call to Miami rung out.

"I see you've been having fun," Michael said, once he heard Alex's voice.

"I've been keeping busy," Alex said. "You?"

"Yes, busy. You're calling about the birthday?"

"Yeah. You going?"

"Of course. We've been summoned. You know, he's going to bring up making another record tomorrow. I just want you to know that it's not me instigating any of that."

"I know," Alex said.

"How are you getting up there?" Michael asked.

"Oh, um, I'm heading up there with a friend," Alex said. "You?"

"I'm driving up there with Epic," Michael said.

"Oh, congratulations by the way. I saw you got him onto *Soul Train.*"

"Yeah, he's going to be huge," Michael said.

"Well, I look forward to meeting him tomorrow."

"Alex?"

"Yeah?"

"No, nothing. I'll see you tomorrow."

At the president's Connecticut estate, Alex and Michael kept a discrete distance from each other until the president made a beeline towards them, calling them into his study to talk business.

"You still owe us two albums," the president said, closing the door behind them and putting his hand on Alex's shoulder.

"I know," Alex said. "I haven't forgotten."

"No don't worry about sitting down boys, I won't keep you long. It's just that I hear there's been some friction. My top selling male artist not happy… that kind of thing. Excuse the frankness."

"It's all in the past," Michael replied.

"I hope so. I'm looking forward to working with you both again. Despite what some of the boys are bragging about outside, no one has been able to fill the space you've left Alex."

"He's already working on ideas," Michael said coolly. Alex only now noticed how much weight Michael had lost. Michael's wavy, dark hair now looked disproportionately large in comparison to his tiny head.

"Yes, don't leave it too long," the president said, looking at Alex. "All that momentum you created will have been for nothing. Mustn't let yourself get too distracted," he said, making Alex uncomfortable. "Anyway, I'm stoked that the two of you made it all the way up here. It's been far too long. Let's not leave it so long between drinks next time," he said, opening the door and ushering them out, accompanying them to the main hall before he headed off on his own.

"Where are you going?" Michael asked.

"Out for a cigarette. I need some air," Alex said, patting down his pockets.

"I'll come with."

Outside they surveyed the green, manicured gardens laid out below them in silence.

"You know Alex," Michael finally said, his eyes on a huge cypress tree in the distance. "It really has been too long."

"I know," Alex said, inhaling sharply.

"I wish I could turn back time. I feel so shitty about how I handled things," Michael said.

"Oh, there you are!" a voice boomed. "You must be Michael," Ferris suddenly said, standing between them and holding out his hand, which Michael reluctantly shook.

"I've been looking for you all over," Ferris said, putting his arm around Alex's shoulder. "What's say we blow this scene? Head back to the city? If we leave now, we'll make it in time for the Tommy Boy party. I hear De La Soul are performing."

"I have to go check on Epic," Michael said, stepping away from them. "See you back in the city?"

But Ferris bundled Alex away before he could respond, quickly dragging him through the guests and tables to the coat check.

Back in New York, they stopped at Ferris' house to get changed. Ferris led Alex into his wardrobe and while Alex began going through the racks, looking for something to change into, Ferris embraced him from behind, unbuckling Alex's belt. He shoved his hand down into Alex's underpants and felt Alex tense up. Ferris then spun Alex around and pulled Alex's trousers down to his knees, sucking away at the lump in white cotton that hovered before him.

Throughout the rest of the spring, their lovemaking sessions remained fast, furious and spontaneous. They fucked in the back of Ferris' town car, in cloakrooms… even behind closed doors at parties, oblivious to the risk of being caught by other guests.

For weeks they wreaked all kinds of havoc across the city. If Alex managed to get Ferris home for the night, Ferris usually left at some point after Alex had fallen asleep. But as summer approached, Ferris began cancelling plans at the last minute, disappearing for days at a time, returning with vague explanations about work in LA or London only to vanish again.

As his absence wore on, the rush of being with someone who refused to capitulate began to wear off for Alex. It frustrated him to no end that he'd failed to learn how to bend what he "had" with Ferris into something that resembled a relationship. And after a month of Ferris being out of contact, the frustration turned to dismay when Alex realised what they "had" was over.

With the realisation, Alex's desire to stay in New York waned. He finally began to concede that he had to go to Miami and begin thinking about the album he was due to make. He had no idea of what he wanted to do lyrically or musically, but he knew it was time to say his goodbyes.

So he organised a lunch, with the intent of letting it evolve into a dinner if his guests felt inclined to stay on. With an assortment of new friends (pretty much all Ferris') in attendance, alongside Xavier, Jasper and their respective partners, Alex gave the order to the serving staff to begin dishing out.

Shortly after the first course had been served, one of the staff discretely conveyed that Ferris was on his way up.

"Did you invite him?" Xavier asked quietly.

"No," Alex said. "I would've but I haven't seen him in weeks."

"Do you want me to handle it?"

"No Xavi," Alex said, standing up, and walking back into the apartment, a mix of excitement and irritation surging through him.

"Whey hey," Ferris said when Alex opened the front door.

"I didn't know you were coming," Alex said.

"Aw, don't be annoyed. I thought I'd surprise you. And you *did* say something about leaving and lunch today in one of the bazillion messages you left me."

"Of course," Alex said. "Everyone's on the deck," Alex added, watching as Ferris discarded his stuff on the floor and walked outside, loudly greeting everybody.

A spot was hurriedly prepared for Ferris beside Alex who nervously took his own spot as the conversation continued.

Ferris ignored Alex throughout the meal, pulling away anytime Alex reached out to touch him under the table or paid him any attention. As the dessert came out, one of the guests recounted an unfortunate experience a friend had with an 8 ball a few nights earlier.

"Must've been a friend of Alex's! Alex must be the only popstar I know who doesn't know what to do with a line of coke," Ferris scoffed, some of the guests laughing nervously at the remark. "He's like a deer in headlights!"

"Don't call me a popstar," Alex replied, to yet more unintentional laughs.

"Of course you're a popstar, darling," Ferris said.

"Don't Ferris," Alex said. "I'm not in the mood."

"What? You're a popstar. You don't need to be embarrassed about it. It's like what all the people at this table do but without any of the depth. Stuff for the masses. Production line stuff. *Somebody's got to do it.*"

"Don't take your shitty week out on me," Alex said tersely.

"What do you know about my week?" Ferris asked.

Alex looked around the table and decided against answering.

"Oh, I see," Ferris said, sitting back in his chair. "You've been talking with one of your pals. Heard what happened, did you?"

"What happened Ferris?" Jasper asked. "Don't be shy. We're all friends here, aren't we?"

Ferris took a swig of his drink while Alex leaned away from him.

"Oh, you don't want to talk about it? Have a run in did you?" Jasper asked, smiling, his lips curling up at their ends.

"Well, no point talking about it with you lot. You wouldn't get it," Ferris said, his British accent suddenly pronounced. "You're blinded to how joyless and dour he and his friends are.

Sycophants!" Ferris said, gesturing madly at everyone but staring at Alex.

"Don't you get tired of surrounding yourself with people who only want to kiss your arse?" Ferris sniped, cocking his head at Xavier who had his arm around Alex's shoulder. "Don't you tire of people fawning over you? Of people buying into this idea that you and your cronies are prophets, just because you all sing and dance? And I use those words loosely! You're all just basically selling the idea of dumbness. None of you are changing the world like you make out you are. The only agenda you and your mates are pushing are your own."

"Jesus, Ferris," Xavier said. "You'd better pull your head in."

"Why? Because you're all afraid of hearing the truth? You're all scared of anyone speaking up and ruffling a few feathers? He...," Ferris said, pointing at Alex, "...he's the worst of them. He sucks you in, drains you of your energy and then expects you to be at his beck and call. And you do it, because you can bask in his spotlight a bit. But he's like a fucking succubus. And when he doesn't get his way, he goes about making your life miserable. Don't you, you little, vindictive popstar?"

"I don't know what you're on about," Alex said.

"Oh no? Didn't call your old mate George? Didn't tell him to drop me from his campaign 'cos I got bored of you and treated you badly?"

"If you got dropped, it's your own doing. Look at you. You're a mess," Alex said, his voice calm even if every one of his nerves was tingling.

"Fucking bullshit!" Ferris spat. "You make yourself out to be holier than thou, but you're not. You're a manipulator."

"Not my fault that you don't know how to handle the pressure. You always want to be the centre of attention, but the minute all eyes are on you, you don't know what to do with yourself," Alex said, his voice hardening. "I had nothing to do with you getting fired from that job. Maybe it was your insecurity. And you're just looking to blame me for it," Alex said, congratulating himself with a sip of his wine.

It was at this point Ferris launched his hands into Alex's face, sending Alex, his chair and the wine glass to the floor. Ferris pounced on him and began landing punches, causing a commotion as Jasper and Xavier dived in to separate them. It took the two of them to drag Ferris back into the apartment, Ferris belligerently gathering his belongings and knocking Alex's knick-knacks over on his way out the front door.

Alex, now on his feet, was in a mild state of shock. He did his best to try and regain his composure, watching as his guests smoothed over the scene and restored order, passing off Ferris' actions as those of a mad man.

Xavier returned with some ice in a napkin which he applied to Alex's cheek.

"He got you off guard there, hey?" he said, rubbing Alex's back.

"I should've just let him blow off steam. I deserved it."

"You didn't. He's a dick. But he needed an audience to prove it. You know, on his way out, he swore black and blue that you were responsible for him getting canned."

"I had nothing to do with it, Xavi," Alex said, putting his hand to his cut lip and inspecting the blood it left on his finger.

"He said that one of his contacts told him it was because someone at Kēvala was laying on the pressure."

"I had nothing to do with it, I swear. I only knew about it because it was in *Variety* this morning."

"Oh," Xavier said. "Well, maybe he was making it all up. The only other person who would drop Kēvala's name is Michael, and why would he bother getting his hands dirty like that?"

"No idea," Alex said, thinking. "Maybe Ferris is just looking for a scapegoat," he added, his nerves tingling again.

| 14 |

ROAD TRIPPING

Ian had been working away on a new batch of music for a musical. The songs were more sophisticated than anything he'd ever come up with, and they were dripping with the sounds of the sixties and seventies. When the musical went up in smoke because its investors backed out of the project, he sent copies of the songs to Alex in New York along with a note asking if Alex had any idea what to do with them all.

In between packing for Miami and leaving countless messages for Ferris in LA and New York, Alex played the tape, the music filling his living area and seeping out onto the deck as he sunbathed. Ian had made more than two dozen recordings, and though they were beautiful, atmospheric songs, at times they were a little too old school for Alex's tastes.

On the day he was due to take his flight to Miami, Alex made a snap decision, quite unlike any he'd ever made before. In the morning he rose early, took his baggage down into the basement and roughly dumped it all into the trunk of his 4WD which he hadn't touched in months. Relieved that it started on the first go, Alex drove himself to the service station on First Avenue where he filled the tank and bought himself a road map.

He sat at the counter, ordering a coffee and some pastries and began to mark out points on the map; places that somewhere in his subconscious, he'd always promised to pass by. He devised a route that he hoped would take him through Tennessee, Oklahoma and New Mexico and then on through to California.

"Hey," he said to the attendant, a man Alex suspected was in his fifties. "What's the best way for me to get to Tennessee from here? I can't make sense of it on the map."

The attendant smiled. "That's a long drive buddy. Would take you at least fourteen hours. You done much driving? Interstate I mean."

"No," Alex said, sipping his coffee.

"Well, you'd best go through Virginia. That way you can stop when you get tired. Show me the map? Ok, see here you need to take FDR and head towards Newark. From there you can take the 78. It'll take you the whole day just to get to Virginia."

"I see," Alex said, following the attendant's instructions.

"You'll be able to make Roanoke by night fall if you make good time. Shouldn't have any problems finding somewhere to stay there."

"Thanks," Alex said. He folded the map away and trawled the store for an assortment of treats and drinks which he sprawled out over the counter. "Can you give me a large coffee to go and two packs of Marlboros as well? And is there a payphone around here?"

"On the lot. Near the air and water."

From the lot he called Ian. "I'm sorry. I woke you."

"What the hell are you doing up so early?" Ian asked, grog-gily.

"I'm not ready. I need some time. I'm completely blanking out. I'm going to take some time out and I'll be in touch. Could be a week or two."

"Ah, okay," Ian grunted. "Wish I'd known earlier. Do Kōji and Celia know?"

"No," Alex said, looking at the traffic piling up in the distance. "I'll call Kōji today to let him know."

"Call him now so he doesn't waste his whole day getting stuff ready for you. I can hear traffic. Where are you?"

"On First Avenue."

"Alex are you alright?"

"Yeah. I'm going on a road trip."

"Oh God. Promise me you'll be careful. You're shit at dri-ving."

"I'll be in touch. I promise."

Driving through the interchanging manmade and natural worlds he switched between his bag of cassettes, the radio and bouts of silence, stopping occasionally to stretch his legs, take a photo, or for fresh air.

Although his confidence grew with each day on the road, he stuck to a major city route, passing through Nashville, Memphis and Oklahoma City, enjoying his anonymity and improvising when asked where he was headed or why he was in town.

When he finally reached New Mexico after a week on the road, he took a detour up to Santa Fe, where he decided to stay a couple of days.

He found a suitably comfortable hotel which he checked into in the afternoon, and after being ushered into a room with a view, he lay down on the bed, coming to the following morning with the first rays of sunlight.

Awaking clear headed for the first time in weeks, he surveyed the room noting the welcome basket of fruit and the lurid violet decor.

'*No more distractions*' he warned himself, hanging the *Do Not Disturb* sign on his door. Plugging in his tape recorder, he pressed play on Ian's tape and began flicking through his notebooks, highlighting lines he'd never harvested, and copying them onto his notepad.

When dusk began to fall and he'd long polished off the last piece of fruit, Alex realised he'd been at it all day. He remotely checked his answering machine hoping Ferris had called to make peace, but his machine was instead full of messages from his management team and concerned friends.

He called Xavier and chatted for a few minutes, before briefly checking in with Kōji, Celia and Ian.

Stepping out into the fresh air after answering the concierge's standard enquiries, Alex ambled around the area near his hotel, spying a diner on his way up to the cathedral. With the cathedral closed, he backtracked to the diner and settled into a corner table by the front windows.

He helped himself to the newspaper on a nearby table and when the plump and smiley waitress came by to take his order, he ordered some vegetarian fare and a Bloody Mary. Nearby there were one or two other customers but it seemed like a quiet night. As he read the national paper, he noticed one of the customers looking at him. It wasn't persistent. Just a glance thrown his way from time to time. After the Bloody Mary arrived, their eyes met, and Alex smiled.

"Engrossing read?"

"Presidential race… hardly anything interesting," Alex answered.

"You're staying at the Inn right? I err, I checked in at the same time as you."

"Oh, right," said Alex. "Yeah, just here for a few days. Passing through."

"Lucky you. I'm stuck here for the week. Not sure what I'm going to do with myself. A few meetings and a lot of free time."

"It's the worst isn't it? Traveling for business. You can never really relax, can you?" Alex asked.

"Yeah. I've been on the road for a month already. Slowly going out of my mind. I'm Gabriel."

"Nice to meet you. Alex."

"Alex, do you want to join me? I mean, I don't want to pull you away from your reading, but it would be nice to have a bit of company."

Gabriel looked like he was in his early thirties or possibly older. Alex couldn't tell. The combination of prematurely grey hair and angular features made it difficult to guess. Handsome, if in that slightly generic way, Alex had already detected an East Coast accent. As Alex took his seat at Gabriel's table, he detected a hint of cologne while clocking Gabriel's matching shoes, belt and watch. Alex suspected he was from Boston, possibly New York, but asked, if only to spur on the conversation.

"Bostoner," Gabriel said. "But I live in Philly."

Their conversation was standard enough, covering off the presidential race, the hotel and even the weather, but more seemed to be said with their exchanging of glances.

After the meal they stayed on for a couple of drinks in the diner with a handful of customers who'd come in for late suppers. It was a weeknight, one of them eventually remembered, accounting for why it was so quiet, at which point the talk turned to New York and their preferred places to hang out at. Gabriel not so subtly named checked a couple of gay bars in amongst his list, Alex understanding the subtext.

"Should I ask for the bill?" Alex asked. "We can grab a night-cap at the hotel if you like?"

After a succession of Tequila shots at the hotel bar, but little in the way of real chemistry, Alex nonetheless invited Gabriel up to his room. As Alex moved his belongings off the bed, Gabriel unbuttoned revealing an alabaster torso and a huge crucifix that hung over it.

"Irish Catholic," Gabriel said, unzipping his fly. "Get on your knees."

The following morning Alex again woke to the daylight streaming in, and, rolling over, found that Gabriel was awake next to him, reading one of his notebooks.

"Morning. Didn't know you were a poet," Gabriel said.

"Just do it to help get myself to sleep," Alex said, irritated Gabriel had helped himself to the journal.

"I've got to go to Albuquerque today, but I'll be back this afternoon. Want to grab dinner when I get back? I know a good hacienda out near Chimayó," Gabriel said, putting his palm on Alex's chest.

"Sure, okay," Alex replied, even if he realised he'd prefer to skip all the pleasantries and simply fuck again like they did last night. Gabriel was a bore but Alex appreciated how well Gabriel had read him sexually. Alex was pleasantly surprised that Gabriel had so convincingly dominated him just as he'd secretly hoped for.

After breakfast Alex toured the downtown area, loosely following the itinerary in the *Historical Walking Map* the eager check in desk staffer had given him. He visited the sandstone cathedral and chapels listed, dawdling around the downtown area until the heat got too uncomfortable. Returning to his hotel, he booked himself a spot on a morning hike and settled down in his room for the afternoon where, once again he went through the motions of listening to Ian's tapes and looking through his notebooks. He kept at it until dusk, stopping only when the phone rang.

"Alex, it's me, Gabriel. Can you be ready in half an hour?"

His head was elsewhere, probably stuck somewhere in his journal pages or in one of Ian's melodies, but on the drive out to the hacienda, Alex did his best to keep the conversation going.

Over dinner, Alex found himself distracted by his writer's block. He lacked the extra energy needed to engage with Gabriel.

"Have I done something wrong?" Gabriel asked.

"No, why?"

"It's just that I feel like you'd rather be anywhere but here."

Alex felt a wave of discomfort wash over him.

"I'm sorry, you're right. I've just got a lot on my mind."

"Messy breakup?" Gabriel asked, smiling.

"That obvious?"

"No," Gabriel said, elongating the word. "The poems. The distraction. On my way back from Albuquerque I worked it out. Why you looked so familiar. Oh, no, don't look at me like that. Your secret is safe with me. I'm not going to say anything."

"It's just been a challenging couple of months," Alex admitted.

"I can imagine. The lyrics... are they for your new record?"

"They should be. But it's not coming along so well."

"They say you can't force that kind of thing," Gabriel said.

Alex felt relief that his "secret" was out and that Gabriel didn't seem to be starstruck.

"No. Not if you want to do something decent," Alex agreed. He finally took a bite of his meal. "The thing is, I'm trying to do something different this time. Don't want to do more of the same anymore."

"But if more of the same works for you, why not?"

"I know. But I'm almost thirty. I feel like I should do something better. That I should have something to say."

"God, you're still a baby," Gabriel said. "Anyway, it's a bit hard to say something if you're always having to hide who you are," Gabriel said. "Worse when you're gay."

"You think?" Alex asked.

"People say things are changing. I don't know about that. I was really nervous yesterday. In Boston or New York, even some parts of Philly, I wouldn't have thought twice about hitting on you. But in places like this, I'm usually way more careful. Or I just look for a beat."

"Well, I'm glad you hit me up yesterday."

"Me too. Had I have known who you were, I probably wouldn't have had the courage. Probably would've just asked you for an autograph."

Alex smiled. He was suddenly warming to Gabriel.

"You got a boyfriend in Philly?"

"Yeah," Gabriel said, to Alex's surprise disappointment.

"Been together long?"

"For years," Gabriel said, finishing his trout. "He's a bit older than me," he added, "and not that interested in sex anymore," he said wiping his mouth with his napkin.

"How old are you by the way?" Alex asked, finally finishing his pequín.

"Forty five," Gabriel said, beaming.

"Jesus, you don't look it."

"Alex, I don't want to rush you, but hurry up and finish your margherita. I want to take you back to my room and fuck the living daylights out of you," Gabriel said, hushed but insistent.

The following morning after a dawn lovemaking encore and his hike, for which he'd disguised himself with a cap and sunglasses, Alex lazed around town, visiting two bookstores while he waited for his hike photos to be processed at the photo shop. That afternoon in his hotel room, some words trickled out as he listened to two of Ian's pieces, but unable to do much more than make notes about the instrumentation, he concentrated on some of the books he'd purchased in the morning.

The following day after waking up in Gabriel's room, Gabriel drove them out to the Cerrillos Hills State Park which they hiked around, abruptly interrupting their walk with some erotic interludes.

"You know I'm kind of relieved I have to leave tomorrow morning," Gabriel said, tucking himself back in.

Alex held up his hand as if to say wait, while he gargled some water. "Why?"

"Because if I hang around any longer, I know I'm going to completely fall for you," Gabriel said, nervously.

Alex looked at him and smiled. "Your boyfriend's a really lucky guy," he said, holding out his hand. "Help me up?"

In Alex's room that night, Gabriel crawled under the sheets.

"I know this is going to sound completely psycho, but could you hold me tonight?" Gabriel said softly. "Try not to fall asleep straight away?"

"Sure," Alex said, pulling the sheets away and cupping his hand behind Gabriel's head. "Just try not to make me come so hard like you always do," he gushed, pushing Gabriel's head down to his groin.

He knew he probably shouldn't have done, but the following morning after taking Gabriel out for breakfast, he gave Gabriel his phone number, telling Gabriel to look him up next time he was in New York.

Once they'd said their goodbyes in a parking lot on the city's outskirts, Alex followed Gabriel's advice and took the I–25, driving south down into Mexico to Juarez. With Jasper's telephone help the night before, Alex managed to locate Andres, a director friend who was working on a film in and around Juarez.

Alex stayed for a couple of days, watching Andres direct scenes on the Samalayuca Dune Fields and hanging by night in the city with his small production crew. Energised after a few nights soaking up the atmosphere, Alex drove back across the border and headed towards California.

Arriving in LA, he took a punt and drove directly to Ferris' place. Tired from the traffic and the long drive, he nonetheless sounded the buzzer at the gates. Getting no response, he drove back to the public phone he'd passed on the way up to the house and tried calling instead, but the line simply rang out. It was a Wednesday night; Ferris could be anywhere.

Driving past the modest (by Hollywood standards) house he'd handed over to Athena, Alex checked into the Waldorf Astoria in Beverly Hills, where he tried Ferris' number a few more times before showering and passing out in the king size bed.

In the morning, the minute he woke, he tried the number again, but there was no response. He backtracked to the house and went through the same process of both buzzing and trying the home number from the phone booth, but nobody answered. Looking at his watch, he decided to head downtown in one final attempt. Leaving his dusty 4WD with the valet, he made his way up to the seventh floor.

"Hi Sarah," he said, alighting from the lift.

"Alex, hi," she said, a little startled, and perhaps embarrassed.

"What's wrong?" he asked.

"It's just a surprise to see you here," she said. "Have you come to see someone from the board?"

"No, I came to see Ferris. I heard he was doing something for you guys."

"Um, he is, but not here. He's back in London. I think he actually picked up and moved. He's been made the director of the offices there."

He could see that she realized she'd winded him with the news. "I'm really sorry. I know I should've replied to your messages. I would've been clearer if I thought you were in LA. It's just... Ferris was really adamant. He said I wasn't to say anything."

"Ah, I see," Alex said, crestfallen.

It was a simple enough explanation. But he just wanted to give up, there and then.

"I'm really sorry. Can I get you something? Do you want some water? You look a little pale."

"No, Sarah," he said, shaking his head. "I'm fine. I must've got my wires crossed. Don't worry about saying anything to him about me having come in."

"Okay," she smiled, making him feel even more a fool.

He drove himself to, well, he didn't know where. He'd been so busy being on autopilot since arriving in LA, that he didn't realise where he was. Perhaps he'd been heading to Malibu out of habit. He pulled the car over, got out and had a cigarette, cussing and swearing like a madman by the sidewalk. He wasn't sure what he should do; whether to head back to his hotel and just try and calm down or get the first flight out to New York or Miami.

He lit another cigarette and to his own bewilderment, started to cry. An embarrassing, gulping cry that he hoped none of the passing drivers noticed.

He couldn't remember the last time he'd cried, and cried so much, but he was sure he'd never experienced his world ending like he was in that moment.

It took longer than he expected but he eventually got a grip of himself. As he regained his composure he got back into his car and headed off again, determined to find his way back to his hotel. There, he fished out his swimming bag from the jeep and headed straight to the pool, swimming lap after lap for an hour, feeling as if each stroke, each kick, was relieving him of some of his anger.

After the swim, he pulled out his lyric book, but after setting it on the table couldn't bring himself to look through it. Instead, he fished out the book he'd bought in Juarez on *The Day Of The Dead*, pulling it out alongside the books on Frida Kahlo, Diego Rivera and Leonora Carrington he'd bought in Santa Fe. He flicked through them for a half hour, sure that they would calm and entice him, but he quickly grew tired of them and made a round of phone calls instead. He simply didn't want to be in his own company any longer.

"I'm home alone tonight," Max said, when Alex told him he was in Beverly Hills. "Jake is in Vancouver filming. Come over. I've got a bottle chilling that you're going to love."

Ever since Alex and Michael had taken Max up on his invitation to stay at his private island at the height of all the *Felicidad* mayhem, Max and Alex had stayed in touch.

"*Alleycats,*" Max said, warmly embracing him at the door.

"It's not like you to answer your own door," Alex said mischievously.

"I sent the help home," Max said, closing the door and ushering Alex through his palatial living area. "Let's go outside. It's lovely tonight."

LA twinkled below them, yet it was cooler out than inside.

"What are you doing in LA?" Max asked, uncorking a bottle.

"I got bored. I've been on a road trip," Alex replied.

"I see. Haven't heard from you in a while. Are those little rumours about a big fight in New York true then?"

"Yeah," Alex said, swirling his glass.

"You don't have to swirl it. The grapes are exquisite. They breathe of their own accord," Max said. "Cheers then."

"It's great, the wine I mean."

Max nodded. "It's a shame, he's a fun guy. But he's not right for you."

"How do you mean?" Alex asked.

"You're all heart *Alleycats*. All heart. Ferris… Ferris is a good time. Fun, but not relationship material. I've seen it with him before. And I've seen you before too. You two, you're not a good match."

"Yeah. The fucked up thing is that I think I love him."

"I'm sure you do. But some people aren't meant to be together. Not good for each other. You and Michael were a good fit. Shame that went the way it did. I really like him."

"I know. I like him too. I just can't be in the same room as him," Alex confessed.

"Still bad? Happens to the best of us," Max said. "Well, now that he's moved on it might make things easier, hey."

Alex studied Max suspiciously for a moment.

"Oh, you didn't know?" Max said.

"No," Alex said, practically shoving his whole face into his wine glass. "Is it Epic?"

"Oh, so you *did* know?" Max said, smiling and topping up their glasses.

Alex stewed in silence.

"You're always testing me. Have you started on the album yet?"

"I'm still stuck. I was supposed to start in Miami a couple of weeks ago."

"You've got a lot riding on this one Alleycats," Max said. "Take your time. Do it properly."

"I don't know if I've got it in me," Alex said, the frustration he'd felt in the morning overcoming him again.

"Ah come on kid, you're going to get through this. Sometimes the forest has to burn before you see it for the trees. Listen, I've got an early morning conference call with Tokyo, so I'll have to call it a night soon. You're welcome to stay of course. Oh and before I forget. I'll be in New York at the end of the summer. If you're there, let's spend some time together."

"Of course," Alex said.

"Don't rush," Max said. "I'm just saying I can't have a late night, that's all."

"I forgot that y'all are all early to bed and early to rise here."

"Stay as long as you want. Stay the night even," Max said. "I could do with your company."

| 15 |

WITHOUT YOU I'M NOTHING

That night, back at his hotel, Alex made a litany of phone calls, making all sorts of arrangements.

He packed his bags and the following morning, called Kōji, giving him instructions on what to do with the car.

"I need you to find me a car hauler," Alex said. "Just make some calls. I'll be leaving the keys with the hotel. Someone needs to take it back to New York."

"Where are you going now? Are you coming to Miami?" Kōji asked, nervously.

"No. I'll be away for a few more weeks. I think I'll be back in time for September."

Shortly after he hung up, the phone rang.

"Good morning sir. Your driver has arrived."

"Great," Alex said, surveying his suite. "Can you send someone up for my things?"

He slept for most of the fourteen hour flight and as promised, an attendant was waiting for him at the airport to shuttle him through to the domestic terminal.

It was good to be back in Australia.

Landing in Melbourne, he instructed his driver to take him into the city centre.

He'd been completely caught by surprise by how under-dressed he was, having forgotten how cold Melbourne winters can be.

In Melbourne, he spent time with his parents but opted to sleep at his warehouse apartment on the edge of the city centre. He'd purchased it shortly after the divorce, and spent a full day dragging his parents around with him, shopping for additional furniture.

While he savoured his time with his parents, he rationed it, preferring instead to disappear to his beach estate for most of the month, batting down the hatches and watching the weather turn foul over the water.

He kept his own hours there, keen to re–enter "the story" of his album which had come to him after hearing something Max had said to him in LA.

Alex revelled in the drudgery of winter, sleeping late and taking afternoon kips, working around the clock on his ideas for lyrics and Ian's music.

Writing a completely new set of lyrics, he was struck by a bittersweet nostalgia and grief for what could've been. He wondered what life might have looked like if he'd stayed in his hometown, or if he'd been able to keep things going with Ferris, Michael or even Athena.

Being back in Australia played with his sense of time and space. He recognised some places and ways of thinking but now found others completely foreign.

Each day he'd take a long walk along the sand, watching as the rough waves crashed into each other, cancelling themselves out. He wished the pressures he felt could do the same thing.

Instead, back at his house, he devised a way to write about his experiences. He decided that there were different kinds of Alexs; *Naïve Alex*, *Cynical Alex* and *Relationship Alex*. He felt by treating himself as a series of personas, he could pinpoint why things had gone wrong and explore what wrongs had been done to him. Slowly, his personas revealed themselves to him, and he set about telling their stories with the help of Ian's music. He cherry picked elements of the instrumentals, and using his keyboard, made his own changes and adjustments to the music.

By late August, after two weeks of solid work, Alex knew he had the structure for his new album, it's title – *Without You I'm Nothing* – coming from one of the *Relationship Alex* songs.

By the time the press had heard the gossip that Alex was hiding out in the coastal town, he was already back in Melbourne to say his goodbyes, and on a flight back to New York when the stories hit the press.

He'd planned for New York to be a flying visit; a chance for him to get things in order before he had to disappear into the Miami studio for months.

But in New York, he received two unexpected calls; one from Max, and another from Gabriel, also in town on business.

Max begged Alex to join him for a lunch with a hotshot film director who had a project that Max was certain Alex was perfect for.

Calling Max back to agree to lunch, Alex also called Gabriel and booked him in for a late dinner.

At The Quilted Giraffe, Alex cut a dashing figure, turning heads as the only celebrity in attendance that day.

Max and Stephen, the director, were already talking when Alex arrived. Once the mains were taken away, Max began with the shop talk. He explained his new production company was financing two films that Stephen had in the pipeline.

"We're about to start filming an ensemble this month, but we're also developing a really interesting script," Stephen said. "It's like an anthology; three stories about New Yorkers at crossroads. In one, there's a dancer at the end of the line. He's ageing out of his career and he has to find a way to parlay his skills into something new."

"And you thought of me for it?" Alex asked, smiling dutifully.

"I want someone who can perform for the camera like its second nature. Someone that can dance. I don't want to use an actor. I want it to be believable," Stephen said.

"Alex," Max interrupted. "Stephen won't be shooting that until the spring. Possibly later. It's all to be done here in New York."

"Alex, it's a role that's made for you. I've seen your music videos. I was watching them again last night as I thought about it. You'd be perfect. It's not a huge role but it's a meaty one, and you'll be able to really sink your teeth into it if you want to. If I send you a script, will you at least read it?" Stephen asked.

"Of course. And thanks. I'm really humbled that you thought of me."

"Actually Max suggested you for it. He said he's never worked with someone as focused and driven as you before. I need someone who'll give it 100%. The dancing is as important as the dialogue."

"I should hire Max as my publicist," Alex said, tapping Max on the shoulder.

"Yeah, maybe you should," Stephen said. "Anyway, I have to dash back to the production offices. There are a few dramas that need to be resolved. Max, I'll call you. Alex, I hope to hear from you soon."

"Seems nice enough," Alex said, once Stephen was gone.

"He's a tyrant," Max said. "But brilliant. What have you got on for the rest of the day?"

"I've got a dinner tonight," Alex said.

"Oh," Max said. "I'd hoped you'd be free."

"Did you have something in mind?" Alex asked.

Max looked at him and winked.

"Oh, Max," Alex said, "come on, we've already talked about that."

"Not even just once?" Max asked. "To make an old friend happy? I've been thinking about you ever since you came around to mine. I can't get you out of my head."

"Max, come on. You know there's all kinds of reasons why we can't."

"Well," Max said, motioning for the cheque. "If your dinner doesn't work out, remember the offer still stands. Who are you seeing tonight anyway?"

"Just someone that's helping me with some ideas for some songs," Alex said.

"Hmm," Max said, handing his credit card to the waiter. "Well, you know where to find me," he said.

At dinner, Alex snuck into the booth he'd reserved for he and Gabriel at Raoul's in Soho, giving Gabriel a long hug and a kiss on the cheek.

"I didn't expect to hear from you," Alex said, sitting down.

"I wasn't planning to be in New York," Gabriel said. "I had some last minute meetings, so I thought I'd take my chances and call. You hungry?"

"Not really," Alex replied.

"Do you mind if I eat? I haven't eaten today," Gabriel asked.

"You kidding? I'll still eat! And I need a drink. You look well."

"Thanks, you too. Haven't seen you all dressed up like this before. Look at you; silk shirt, necklace, hair slicked back. You look a million bucks."

Alex grinned as he looked at the menu. "How long are you in town for?"

"I'm catching the train back tomorrow morning."

"Oh, a lightning visit," Alex replied.

"Sure is. God, you look good Alex." Gabriel shook his head. "I didn't think you'd return my call," Gabriel confessed.

"Why wouldn't I have?"

"Ah you know. What happens in New Mexico, stays in New Mexico."

"I like you Gabriel. Like the way you talk. Like how you listen. Like a lot of things about you that I won't go into. I don't want to make you blush."

"Bloody Mary tonight?" the waiter asked Alex, interrupting apologetically.

"No, a gin and tonic, Eddie. Eddie, this is Gabriel," Alex said, gesturing.

"Hi Gabriel. What would you like to drink?"

"A scotch on the rocks, thanks," Gabriel replied, waiting for Eddie to leave.

"You're on a first name basis with them," Gabriel observed.

"The food's good and the staff are nice. Plus no one bothers me here."

"How's the writer's block?"

"Okay, I think. The mind's ticking again."

"Great. You must be relieved. And the rest of your trip? How did that go? How was Mexico?"

"It was great. I'd like to go back," Alex replied, cocking his head slightly, keen not to divulge anything else about the road trip. "I don't plan on doing any more driving anytime soon, though. How's your boyfriend? Whose name escapes me right now, I'm sorry," Alex said, cringing with embarrassment.

"*Mark.* Mark's fine," Gabriel answered.

"Good, I'm glad," Alex said.

"Yeah, it looks like we've covered all the pleasantries now," Gabriel added, allowing himself a little chuckle.

"Maybe I'm just a bit nervous," Alex said. "It happens."

Eddie arrived with the drinks and disappeared again after taking their orders.

"Don't stress Alex. I'm not here trying to make this more than it is," Gabriel said, smiling to put Alex at ease. "Although, I do plan on going home with you tonight."

"You know what?" Alex said, raising his glass, "We should toast. To the element of surprise," he said, clinking his glass.

***

Kōji had clearly pulled out all the stops in finding Alex a rental in Miami. Had Alex known how beautiful the property was, he may have never embarked on his cross country and intercontinental journeys over the summer. The fact that it had sat unused but paid for out of his own pocket for months irritated Alex somewhat. He knew he should be more careful with his spending as a matter of principle.

For much of September, his days in Ian's studio felt like a rehearsal. They never once switched on the equipment, instead setting up camp around Ian's baby grand piano in the living room, where they workshopped the changes Alex wanted to make to the music.

In a bid to modernize the sound, Alex routinely played out the music on an acoustic guitar, and Ian an electric one, Peter occasionally accompanying them on the piano as they tested the raft of changes.

When they deemed the songs ready for recording, the song camp moved to a commercial studio in Little Haiti, on Michael's insistence. He felt Alex needed the pressure of a professional setting to begin making up for lost time, the album now three months behind schedule.

The first two weeks in Little Haiti proved fruitful, but soon enough the recording sessions began to stretch out, the hired musicians sitting around as they waited out Alex's digressions into the corridor to take phone calls, and later, his disappearances out into the tiny parking lot.

Initially Ian paid little attention to what was happening outside the control room. He did his best to persevere and keep the project running, putting the musicians through their paces, even if it meant they'd have to redo everything once Alex, angry and belligerent from his run–ins outside, would return, upset that they'd gone ahead without him.

Ian was confident that what they were working on was extraordinary, but he knew that the only chance they had in pulling it off, was if Alex was completely onboard for the entire process.

So, it was only after weeks of interruptions and unnecessary downtime that Ian finally left his post during one of Alex's scenes outside the studio. He barged out of the studio yelling Alex's name and was shocked when outside, in the drizzle, he found Alex in the middle of a screaming match with Ferris. Afraid that they were about to come to blows, he wedged himself in between the two of them, tussled by both as their war of words waged on. It took the arrival of Peter some minutes later to finally bring calm to the situation, Ian dragging Alex back into the studio and Peter shepherding Ferris off the lot, warning Ferris that he would call security.

That afternoon, a furious Ian sent all the musicians packing and instructed the reception staff to lock down the control room from outside.

"What, you're going to hold me hostage now?" Alex asked.

"I've known you for the better part of ten years now," Ian said. "And I've never wanted to walk away from you. Ever."

"But you do today?" Alex sniped.

"Alex, all this drama… there's a time and place for it if you really can't do without it. This is not the time or place. You're wasting my time, Peter's time, not to mention the engineer's and the band who I've had to send home. If this keeps going on I'm walking away. And if I have to, I'll speak to my lawyers about blocking what we've already come up with."

Alex looked at Ian angrily as Ian continued.

"You can't keep putting me in this situation. I've put the last four months of my life on hold for you. I never expected that kind of treatment. Not from you at least."

Alex tucked his chin into his chest, thumping away at the armrests of his chair. He began to make guttural noises which alarmed Ian.

"Alex. You need to walk away from him."

"I have," Alex spat.

"Then why's he here? Answer me."

"Because he wants another chance."

"And are you planning on giving him one?"

"I don't want to. But I think after everything that's happened, I'm still in love with him."

"And what about this? Your album? Our future? Do you plan on committing to any of it anytime soon?"

"I do," Alex said. "I do. But it's turning out to be my divorce album isn't it?" Alex asked, shaking his head.

***

There was real relief the week before Christmas, when after sheer commitment and twelve hour days in the studio, they completed the ninth song for the project. Only three remained.

"Alex it's for you. It's Celia," said Peter, handing him the phone.

Celia had taken on Alex's day to day management, while Michael focused on Epic's burgeoning career.

"How are you doing hon?" she asked.

"I'm okay. I'm looking forward to a break," he said. "It'll be my first Christmas in Miami."

Celia made an affirmative grunt. "Listen, you know Michael just got back to New York today, right?" she said.

"Yeah. And? Is he alright?"

"Well you know what he's like after he's been in Puerto Rico with his family. And he took Epic with him this time."

Alex didn't say anything, but Celia continued talking nonetheless.

"Anyway, he's been in the New York office this morning. You know we always get a lot of looneys calling."

"Is it Ferris again?" Alex asked.

"No, the staff know what to do if he calls. Usually we tell them not to pay any attention to the unsolicited calls. But someone's been calling almost daily there for the last month. It's possible it could be serious."

"I don't understand," Alex said.

"The caller swears she works at St. Vincent's in New York."

"And what does she want?"

"She won't say. Says she'll only speak to you," Celia said.

"And the number checks out?" Alex asked.

"It seems to," Celia replied.

"Give it to me then."

It took Alex three days to reach the woman. She'd apparently been rostered off.

"Is that Alex?" she asked, suspiciously.

"Yes. Is that Anne? I hear you've been trying to reach me. What's this all about?"

"I have been trying to reach you. For more than a month now."

"I'm sorry, I only received the messages the other day," Alex said. "Why have you been trying to reach me?"

"I'm a nurse here at St. Vincent's. I've been calling on behalf of a patient."

"Who?"

"Mr. Cohen."

"I'm sorry Anne, but I'm not sure I know a Mr Cohen," Alex said, apologising again.

"No, don't hang up," Anne pleaded. "Maybe there's been a misunderstanding. Which is strange. Mr Cohen is still very lucid. His full name is Benjamin Arthur Cohen."

Alex suddenly felt clammy. "*Ben?*" he asked, desperately.

"Yes. He says he would like to see you."

***

Alex was led along the snaking corridors, the pastel walls and the lines painted on the floor leaving him further disorientated. The doctor seemed nice enough but like everyone else, had no more ideas of what could be done for Ben or how much longer he had.

She had tried to prepare Alex. Ben was "gravely ill" and there was no disguising it. She'd warned Alex how distressing it would be to see him. When she led him into the room Ben was sleeping.

"Buzz if he needs anything," she said, turning away.

It didn't seem like Ben. Nothing of Ben's old stocky physique remained and the way he slept now looked different to the way Alex remembered he did. Ben's face and arms were bony, his skin yellowish and he seemed sunken and hollow in the white sheets.

Alex sat and took Ben's hand, carefully, so as not to wake him. It was cold, its fingers bony. Alex recognised the marks, the Kaposi's sarcomas that had taken root at various points on the body.

For years Alex had lost friends to various forms of the disease or its complications. For years he'd used his profile to be an activist and a public ambassador for HIV/AIDS research, urging people to practice safe sex, quietly donating millions to the cause. Only his accountants would be able to tell him how much, but he'd given over entire proceeds from concerts and singles in addition to his personal donations. Yet the lives of his friends had been taken anyway.

Ben slept for hours, Alex holding his hand the whole time. On her second visit during her rounds, a nurse slipped Alex a juice box, warning him not to become a martyr.

Shortly after seven pm, Ben finally opened his eyes. Finally, Alex recognised something in Ben; the glint in his eyes which shined defiantly from behind his skeletal features.

"*Lekke*," Ben murmured, using the pet name he'd often used for Alex.

"Hi babe," Alex said, smiling. "Long time no see."

Ben managed to converse for a few hours with Alex, who attended to him and helped clean up and change the sheets when Ben had an unexpected bowel movement. With the nurse's permission, Alex gave Ben a sponge bath and crept into the bed, spooning Ben until Ben fell asleep again. That night, Alex returned to his apartment but didn't get to sleep until the wee hours.

The following morning, he made a detour to a bodega before making his way to St. Vincent's. Arriving in Ben's room, he was pleasantly surprised.

"Ah, you're awake."

"*Lekke.* You're back."

"Of course," Alex said. "Considering we missed Hanukkah, we're just going to have to celebrate Christmas this year," Alex said, giving Ben a kiss and then rifling through the bodega bags.

"Did you bring some champagne?"

"I wanted to bring you some Cristal but all they had left was this Kosher stuff," Alex said.

"I'd rather die," Ben said.

"I'm joking. I brought some Cristal, just like I promised. And something else. Here."

Alex placed the package on Ben's midriff and Ben wasted no time in opening it.

"Oh, Yatagan! My old favourite," Ben said, chuckling. "Can you help me with it? Yeah, put your finger on mine, yes, now push," Ben said, Alex obeying and winding up equally doused in the cologne as Ben was.

"Thank you Alex. Did you manage to get the other things too?"

"Yes, I gave them to your doctor. I quite like her you know," Alex said, kissing Ben's forehead.

"Yeah, Leah is a good shiksa," Ben said aloud, relieved that Alex had confirmed he was bankrolling Ben's healthcare and that he'd given Leah the authority to source the supplementary medications.

"You're such a good goyim."

"Ben when did you go all Yiddish?"

"I think it was sometime between me fainting and going into a coma," Ben deadpanned.

"Oh, my little dreidel," Alex said, pouring some Cristal into the paper cup and gently handing it to Ben. "Drink up otherwise the nurses will steal it."

Alex saw in the new year by Ben's bedside, only heading over to the party at Xavier's once Ben fell asleep.

"How is he doing?" Xavier, asked, letting Alex in and kissing him on the cheek, Alex playfully pulling the strap of Xavier's party hat.

"Who knows? He's about to start on the AZT. Fingers crossed," Alex said, accepting a flute of champagne from Xavier's girlfriend.

"When do you have to leave for Miami?"

"Tomorrow, but I'll be back on Friday," Alex said.

"Jasper told me he's going to drop in on him while you're gone," Xavier said. "But that he didn't want you to know."

"Ah, is he here?" Alex asked.

"He was, but he left for some other party in the Village."

When Alex returned to New York he stopped in at St. Vincent's on the way back from the airport, finding Ben tired, but in good spirits.

"I'm glad you and Jasper are still friends after all this time," Ben said. "It was a nice surprise seeing him."

"Oh, he managed to pop by in the end?" Alex said, relieved.

"Every day. He's such a good guy. I'm surprised you two never got together."

"I think we would've strangled each other," Alex said.

"Well it's nice to have friends that you can rely on."

"You've got us to count on now Ben," Alex said.

"I know," Ben said. "You've no idea how much that means."

Leaving the hospital that day, the hair on the back of Alex's neck tingled, Alex feeling like someone was watching him as he got into the cab.

The following morning, there were photographers waiting for him as he left his building, and more waiting for him at St. Vincent's. Though he couldn't hear anything they said on his way in, on his way out later that evening there were many more than there had been in the morning, yelling at him and asking all sorts of questions.

The coming and going from Miami to New York and the bedside vigil continued until the recording of the album was deemed complete and it was finally sent off for mastering. Alex instructed Kōji to ship his personal belongings back to New York and flew off to LA to meet with Andres, Jasper's director friend, who Alex had asked to direct the video for *Paean*, the album's lead single.

After such a lengthy absence, Alex's management team insisted on a big budget, dramatic video to regain the public's attention. But Alex was having nothing of it, and instead worked closely with Andres on the treatment.

"If you could film this anywhere, which I assume you can," Andres asked, "where would you film it?"

Alex thought for a moment. "New Mexico. Or somewhere similar."

"Okay," Andres said. "That will work. But you have to drop the idea of the face paint. You can't go out making yourself to be Native American," Andres said, exasperated, adding a firm "*no*" when Alex attempted to insist otherwise.

Back in New York Alex marshalled Kēvala to put its full resources behind Andres and the planning of his new album's promotional campaign, putting him at loggerheads with Michael who was immersed in Epic's promotion, Epic having finally landed the first of what would be a string of top ten hits for the label.

As Michael and Alex clashed over priorities, Celia quietly redistributed the workloads across their ten staff, allocating half to Michael's needs and the other half to Alex's.

With so much to do in so little time, little attention was paid to the tabloids which burned with accusations that Alex was HIV positive and undergoing treatment in New York. The rumours were creating a maelstrom of public debate and commentary. Alex ignored them and the inflammatory comments of the press who pestered him on the streets of New York as he dashed between business meetings and his daily visits to Ben.

"You're in the papers again," Ben said. "Apparently you've got AIDS and you don't know how long you've got left. Did you know?" he asked, handing Alex a copy of the tattered newspaper.

"They've been following me around constantly since I got back," Alex said. "They'll get tired of it. Something else will come up to keep them busy."

"You should make a statement," Ben said.

"And give them what they want? No." Alex said, kissing Ben as he did and taking his seat on the armchair.

"They've been snooping around here. Security kicked a couple of them out yesterday."

"Comes with the territory. Have they been bothering you?"

"No, but the nurses are a bit pissed with me."

"I'll smooth things out with them. Listen, I've got to go away for a bit. For work."

"The video? Good, I'm glad. I can't wait to hear everything and see it."

"Is the medication working?" Alex asked, pouring moisturiser into his hands and rubbing it into Ben's as he always did.

Ben sighed. "They don't know yet. I just know that I'm more tired than ever now that I'm on it."

"I'll be back soon enough," Alex said, lifting Ben's sleeve and applying the lotion onto Ben's bony upper arms. "I'm going to speak with Leah and see if we can get you out for a night. We're planning a launch for the album."

Ben smiled. "Oh, I haven't been out of this ward in months. I haven't seen you on stage since you were at Madison Square Gardens."

"You were there?" Alex asked, pulling Ben forward and beginning on Ben's back.

"Yep. With Jose, God rest his soul."

"I practically shat myself the first night," Alex chuckled.

"You were fine," Ben said, leaning back into his pillow. "Don't do my legs today. I'm feeling a bit cold."

"Alright," Alex said, tucking the linen back in.

"*Lekke?*"

"Yeah?"

"I love you," Ben said, his voice thin and runny.

"I love you too," Alex replied, kissing Ben's forehead.

***

On location in Albuquerque, Andres' team set to work on the music video.

The narrative had been reduced down to a simple story which cast Alex as a kind of medicine man living on the edge of society. Conceived in three intertwined sequences; one in an old vaudeville theatre, one on Abiquiu Lake and another on a private ranch they'd hired in the desert, Andres was given five days to realise the video.

With an eye on the unpredictable weather, Andres flipped the schedule, choosing to film all the outdoor scenes first.

While the threat of rain held off, the constantly changing light wreaked havoc, made worse by daily temperatures topping out at 13 degrees Celsius.

Alex's costume for the outdoor sequences was so lightweight that he spent the entire time shivering on camera, Andres even instructing his cameramen to zoom in and document Alex's goosebumps.

But watching the playback, the cold and discomfort was worth it, Andres' team capturing evocative and eerie images of Alex on horseback, in a canoe and running through the arid and ruggedly beautiful landscape as he tried to escape the mob of extras.

When production moved back to Albuquerque, filming in the KiMo, an old theatre with a chequered past, Alex performed to camera, backed by a wedding band Andres' team had found to play the musicians.

A still photographer captured Alex's new look; barefoot in corduroys, with an old school vest over his bare chest. His hair, now longish and a mix of brown and auburn, was shellacked with a middle part, his eyes outlined with his trademark kohl.

When shooting wrapped, Alex maintained a fulltime presence in the LA editing room, working alongside Andres and the editing team in a bid to walk away completely satisfied with the film clip. After signing off, the still images taken in the KiMo were sent off to the press in the first salvo in the album's promotion.

Whilst there was excitement at Kēvala and the parent label, there was also great uncertainty. Alex had delivered a quality album, but as was the case with the video, striking as it was, there was fear amongst Alex's management and the sales teams that Alex had moved into radically different territory.

They worried his fans would not be onboard for such a huge change in direction. Alex ignored the tepid response, summoning Ian and many of the album's musicians to New York to begin rehearsals for the album's planned launch. Between hospital visits and rehearsals, Alex began to field interviews with the press, who it seemed were as equally interested in his HIV status as they were in the profound change in his sound which they uniformly referred to as the most "ground-breaking, ambitious and organic sounding music" he'd recorded to date.

As rave advance reviews hit the press, a dance remix of *Paean* was prepared, it serviced to clubs alongside the radio version in February 1989, and on February 24, to coincide with the release of the *Paean* video, Alekzandr launched the album with a performance of seven of its songs for the international press and dozens of his friends at New York's Beacon Theatre, Ben among them.

Alekzandr, kitted out in his new trademark look, tore through the punchy, tight set that he and Ian had put together.

Enjoying being back on stage for the first time in almost eighteen months, he regularly broke into chitchat between numbers, the footage from the show then edited into the dozen or so television interviews he sat down for in the days that followed.

As the hype machine kicked into full gear, and the press' interest in him exploded, Alex resisted calls to travel away from New York.

Ben's health was suddenly declining, and as the public and the media lapped up Alex's new material, lavishing it with praise, Alex spent entire days at St. Vincent's largely oblivious to the hysteria his confessional album was generating.

On Tuesday, March 28, he woke to the high pitched squealing of the fax machine in his corridor. *Paean* it read, was officially No.1 in the US and UK charts, and the album had debuted at No.1 in more than a dozen countries, including Australia.

That morning, his phone rang off the hook, friends and peers calling to congratulate him, but only one caller truly stopped him in his tracks. The shiksa doctor.

"Hi Leah, I'm coming in at the usual time today. Do I need to bring him anything?"

"Alex. I'm sorry, I don't know how to say this. Ben passed away in his sleep this morning."

"No. That can't be," he responded. "I just saw him last night. He seemed fine. Tired, but fine."

"I know. It only happened about an hour ago."

"No Leah, no. That doesn't sound right. I would've known."

"I'm really sorry. I wanted to tell you myself."

Alex watched as another fax spilled out from the machine, making an incessant robotic racket as it did so. He waltzed over and kicked it onto the floor, sending it down with a giant thud.

"What was that? Is everything ok?" Leah asked.

"Just fine," Alex replied.

"Alex, he left you some things. Look, I can organise for them to be sent over for you if you like."

"I can't come and see him? To say goodbye?" he asked, crying.

"He didn't want that," she said sadly. "You know that."

"What am I supposed to do without him?" he asked.

"I don't know," Leah finally said. "You made a huge difference to him. He was so proud of you. You gave him something to look forward to each day. I saw the change in him. The calm he reached. Remember him, that's all you can do."

When a courier arrived at Alex's a few days later, it was clear that Ben had prepared for the moment.

Inside the package were two wooden boxes. One full of valuables: jewellery, things Alex assumed Ben had inherited from his parents, and the other box full of letters that Ben had written but never sent to Alex.

The envelopes all had stamps on them, Alex barely remembering any of their designs. There were dozens of letters, and it took him months to build up the courage to read them, to read of events in Ben's life, and occasionally of Ben's regrets about how their relationship had ended so abruptly.

Amongst the envelopes were a series of Polaroid photos and photo booth prints of the two of them and some other friends. Alex wept, but smiled as he looked through them. There were dozens of the absurd shots they used to take before and after his performances or randomly on the streets of London and New York.

Alex wasted no time in having a large, multi–panelled frame made for the 64 photos, hanging it on his living room wall the moment it arrived back from the framers.

It took Alex years to look at it without wincing or wondering what could've been.

And though Alex would have other lovers, he never once so much as entertained the idea of removing the frame or Ben from its rightful place above the mantle.

ALSO AVAILABLE:

The Nineties: Vinyl Tiger 2nd Edition
The Noughties, Vinyl Tiger 2nd Edition

EXPLORE THE MUSIC AND IDEAS OF THE EIGHTIES FURTHER.

Writing *pop fiction* is only possible with a healthy dose of cultural references. Here's a list of the main artists and cultural references found in *The Eighties*: be sure to check them out!

Iggy Pop and the Stooges, Blondie,

Buzzcocks, Grace Jones,

Andrea True, Joni Mitchell,

Sex Pistols, David Bowie

Lata Mangeshhar, Manna Day

"Nocturnes for the King of Naples" by Edmund White

"Maurice" by E.M. Forster

Simon Le Bon, Duran Duran,

Boy George, Culture Club, Marilyn

Michael Hutchence, INXS

Cocteau Twins, Dead Can Dance

Hall & Oates, Wham!

Michael Jackson & The Jackson Five,

Madonna, Prince

The Cure, The Stalin, Shonen Knife

The Eurogliders, I'm Talking

Nik Kershaw, Howard Jones, Billy Idol

De La Soul

A NOTE TO THE READER

Thanks for being such an indie superstar by reading this!

As an independent author, your feedback and comments are particularly valuable to me.

You can share your thoughts with me via the ways listed below, but one of the most powerful ways to help any independent author – and your fellow readers – is to consider leaving a review for the book you've just read.

Your reviews can make a huge difference in other people discovering the work of indie authors.

In any case, thanks for revisiting the eighties (the decade I discovered music) with me.

Join me on Alekzandr's journey into the Nineties!

ABOUT THE AUTHOR

Melbourne born Dave Di Vito has spent much of his adult life on the run, chalking up stints in London, Lecce and Kyoto.

A former gallerist/curator and trained artist, Dave has been teaching and writing in the Eternal City for more than ten years and now considers himself a fake Roman.

A lover of pop and pop culture, Dave writes pop fiction.

Connect with him via:

Facebook at www.facebook.com/vinyltiger

Twitter @ddvinyltiger

Or **subscribe** to his mailing list for (very occasional!) updates at: https://www.paperlesstiger.net/presscontact

ACKNOWLEDGEMENTS

Vinyl Tiger has been haunting me for years. It came into being via scribbled, handwritten notes on Japanese subways, bumpy bus rides in Rome and during downtime in Melbourne art galleries.

It lived on despite the master copy being stolen in a home break in and its author relocating across three different continents.

With the huge shifts in the way we look at popular culture that have taken place since *Vinyl Tiger* was first published in 2016, this second edition is the result of revisiting the story with fresh eyes.

I appreciate all the help I've received along the way, particularly from Lucy and Shane who helped so much with the first edition, and to my dear Kekks who, more than anybody else, really championed me sitting down and seeing this through.

To my dear, dear family and friends, thanks for putting up with me while I insist on living my bicontinental fantasy.

To the artists of the eighties; brilliant and ridiculous, a huge thank you to you for the inspiration.

And to those who of you who have taken the time to read and discover my work, my heartfelt thanks.

Love,

Dave